Jane Gardam has won two Whitbread awards (for *The Queen of the Tambourine* and *The Hollow Land*). She was also a runner-up for the Booker Prize with *God on the Rocks*, which was made into a much-praised TV film. She is a winner of the David Higham Award and the Royal Society of Literature's Winifred Holtby Prize for her short stories about Jamaica, *Black Faces, White Faces*, and *The Pangs of Love*, another collection of short stories, won the Katherine Mansfield Award. *Going into a Dark House* won the Macmillan Silver Pen Award. In 1999 she was awarded the Heywood Hill Literary Prize for a lifetime's commitment to literature. Her novel *Old Filth* was shortlisted for the Orange Prize in 2005.

Jane Gardam was born in Coatham, North Yorkshire. She lives in a cottage on the Pennines and in East Kent, near the sea.

JANE GARDAM

The Sidmouth Letters

ABACUS

First published in Great Britain by
Hamish Hamilton Ltd in 1980
Published by Abacus in 1981
This edition published by Abacus in 1997
Reprinted 2000, 2007, 2008, 2010 (twice), 2011, 2014

'Hetty Sleeping' first appeared in *Woman* (1977)
'Transit Passengers' first appeared in *Company* magazine (1977)
and in *Is Anybody There?* (Penguin Books, 1978)
'Lunch with Ruth Sykes' first appeared in *Family Circle* (1977)

A CIP catalogue record for this book
is available from the British Library.

ISBN 978-0-349-11408-8

Printed and bound in Great Britain by
Clays Ltd, St Ives plc

Papers used by Abacus are from well-managed forests
and other responsible sources.

MIX
Paper from
responsible sources
FSC
www.fsc.org   FSC® C104740

Abacus
An imprint of
Little, Brown Book Group
100 Victoria Embankment
London EC4Y 0DY

An Hachette UK Company
www.hachette.co.uk

www.littlebrown.co.uk

To Julia MacRae

Contents

Contents

The Tribute

Fanny Soane rang Mabel Ince and Mabel Ince rang old Lady Benson to say that poor Dench was dead.

'Who?' screamed Nelly Benson.

'Dench.'

'Dench?'

'Yes. Poor darling Denchie.'

'Thought she'd died years ago. Must have been a hundred.'

'Nonsense, Nelly.'

'She was old in the War.'

'She was *wonderful* in the War.'

'Wonderful means old. I've been wonderful for years.'

'Nelly –,' Mabel was hoping to be brief. Calls cost money. She was ringing Kensington from Berkshire. Certainly after six o'clock, but still –

'Nelly, I think we ought to do something, Put in a tribute –'

'*The Times* has gone. No sense in a tribute. No tributes now. Nobody getting born. Getting married. Getting tributes. Or dying – more's the pity.'

'Well, Dench has died.'

'In *The Telegraph* I suppose?' . . .

'Yes. Nelly –'

'Sorry. Can't go on. Too expensive.'

'But Nelly, I'm the one who's paying –'

But Kensington, like Dench, died.

Dear Fanny, wrote Mable next, I rang Old Nelly Benson but she's daft as a brush and didn't seem the least bit interested in poor dear Dench. What do you think? I'm quite ready to do something – just a short one. In *The Telegraph* which I suppose is the paper Dench would have wanted now *The Times*

1

seems to have gone for good. Oh dear, I hope Dench went before *The Times.* D'you remember how she always read it smiling? I don't think she could have borne life without the Court Circular. 'It *rivets* me,' she used to say, 'Rivets me.' Though lately I gather she hadn't been well and hadn't been reading anything any more. The last Christmas card I had a year or so ago was very shaky. In fact I seem to remember there was only a signature and the little message was written in by some niece.

Did you by the way get a sort of begging letter about Dench? That was from the niece too, but I didn't keep the address. I always wished I could have done something. She wanted to get poor D. into a private nursing home. Did you do anything? I feel a bit dreadful about it and if we could do this tribute now I think I'd feel a bit better. Shall we ring round? There must be half a dozen families who would want to come in on it. I can think of three Denchie nannied myself.

Dear Mabel,

Oh my dear – I could have told you Nelly Benson is impossible now. Quite batty. She must be absolutely gaga not to want to go in with a tribute – or it's kindness to think so – when one knows how much Denchie did for those awful children, and grandchildren too come to that, for simply years. She saw the famous Charlotte through virus pneumonia you know. Nelly just went off to Geneva to join Charles and left Dench to it. And it wasn't as if Dench was ever paid or anything. At least I never paid her, did you? Just her keep. Well, you just couldn't. She never asked. Poor as a church m. I'd guess. But being a gent – Dench I mean – one just fed her. She 'came to stay'. To 'stop' as she called it, bless her.

Yes, I did get a letter from some niece and I meant to answer it and send a fiver or something but it was just before we went to Penang. I felt a bit awful when I remembered about it long afterwards – too late because I'd lost the address by then, too. I do rather hate that kind of letter. Embarrassing all round. You don't feel you can possibly do enough and so you do nothing. Now of course like you we have just the Service pension. My dear, we need a whip round for *ourselves* now. Wish *we* had a niece!

2

Yes, of course I'll go in with a tribute. If we get say three more people it won't kill us. It's about two pounds a line I think. Something like 'In Memory of dear "Dench", beloved Nannie and friend for many years of . . .' and names of families. Will you get in touch with the rest or shall I? I suppose it shouldn't come to more than, say, 75p each?

The telephone rang in Berkshire and Mabel Ince heard a lot of muttering about tangled wires and then old Lady Benson.

'I've had a letter. From some niece. Hello?'

'Hello? Yes? Nelly? What niece?'

'Old Dench's . . .' peep, peep, peep, peep.

'Nelly, are you in a phone box? Hello?'

'Yes. It's in the hall. To stop the lodgers. She wants to meet us . . . ' peep, peep, peep.

'Nelly, for goodness sake! Can't you put in a ten?'

'Hello. Tuppences are better. You get too long with a . . . ' peep, peep, peep.

'Hello?'

'. . . to meet us with some things old Dench left us. In her will. Wants to meet us . . .' peep, peep.

'Can you write? Can't you write about it, Nelly?'

'. . . on Thursday. Fortnum and Mason's.'

'Fortnum and – Nelly, *would* you write?'

'I *could* write,' peep, peep, peep.

'Whether she'll back out of it of course,' said Mabel, 'is another matter. She says she's not been out of the house for years.'

It was Thursday morning – Thursday fortnight morning, for this was not precipitate. Mabel had set forth from Newbury by car leaving Humphrey with the television and a tray, and picked up Fanny Soane. Together they were now proceeding to Kensington and Nelly Benson. It was not as early in the morning as Mabel would have liked as she had lost time looking for Fanny's house which, being in a maze of identical streets and in Raynes Park and not Wimbledon as she had been led to believe, had proved illusive. Fanny's husband in a darned cardigan had seen them to the door as they left, waved perfunctorily and disappeared. His eyes, which as attaché in Tiflis had

3

been interestingly hooded, now had deep swags beneath them, suggesting gin. He was losing his hair. The tiny front garden Mabel noticed had been put down to Brussels sprouts, and an elephant's foot, converted to a boot scraper, stood near the mat.

'A far cry from the Lion Palace,' said Fanny noticing Mabel noticing. 'Sometimes I wonder why we didn't Stay On – though when you read that funny little man –'

'Funny little man?'

'The one who wrote *Staying On*. The one who came out to India for five minutes and wrote all those huge books about us though goodness knows how. I never met a soul who knew him, did you?'

'At least,' said Mabel, 'Dench never knew. What's become of us all I mean. She was such a romantic. She talked about "love of country", d'you remember? Actually used the words. And d'you remember how she stood for the Queen?'

'Oh well, we all did that. We still do. Don't you?'

'Well – not to make it obvious. It depends where we are. And not like Dench did, to attention – quite eccentrically really as if it was almost a joke. Humphrey and I just sort of hesitate now – getting the coats from under the seat. We just stop talking for a moment.'

'Like vicars wondering about Grace when you ask them to dinner.'

'*Do* you ask vicars to dinner?'

'No. Well I don't know that we ever did. We don't ask anybody to dinner now. Can't afford it. Nobody asks us – we're all in the same boat. I mean the people who ask us to dinner now are not the sort one knows. Spaghetti bolognese and cheesecake.'

The two women looked back on half a life-time of invitations – battlefields, of notes, menus, first guest lists second guest lists all professionally conceived, negotiated, carried through. Jousts, tournaments, ritual murders – masked by smiles and decorations.

'D'you remember the Bensons' invitations?'

'Lord yes – "gloves"! Bottom left-hand corner, "gloves will be worn". Poor Nelly.'

'D'you remember Prague? The high ceilings? So beautiful.

4

Somebody told me the other day why embassy ceilings are always so high. It's to take the noise of the cocktail parties.'

'I'd have thought Prague was older than cocktail parties.'

'Nothing's older than cocktail parties. Of one kind or another. Didn't old Dench love cocktail parties? And Prague? I used to let her stand with the children just out of sight on the landing – the Ambassador was so good about Staff – and watch all the people. The children were such angels with Dench.'

'And she *had* them so beautiful.'

'Oh yes. My word she must have cost us something. I mean H.M. Government something. Those little dresses – always Harrods or The White House. The smocking always going round across the back. Round-toed shoes. Like little conkers!'

'Oh – and the herring-bone tweeds! With the little velvet collars – Mabel, I'm going to cry. Dear old Dench. Didn't she iron and press well?'

They picked up Lady Benson rather uncertainly at an address near Notting Hill, not at first recognising her. The house was dilapidated with dirty window panes, the upper floors partitioned down the middle of windows with plaster-board and covered with stickers saying 'Capital Radio' and 'I Still Love Elvis'. A grubby-looking woman peered from a downstairs front room and turned out to be Lady Benson herself, ungloved. She appeared on the top step wearing bedroom slippers and carrying a leather shopping-bag. Her hair was extremely untidy and a smell of onions which hung about the hall accompanied her. There was still an imperial look to the eyes.

'You're not going to Harrods in bedroom slippers, Nelly!'

'I thought it was Fortnum and Mason's?'

'No – we changed it. Harrods is less flashy. But you'd hardly go to Fortnums –'

'They're all I can get my feet into, except wellingtons. I don't go about much now. I have the house to run.'

Big flakes of plaster had come away from around the rain-water pipes. The desolate February garden was full of broken, purple edging-stones and dead hydrangeas.

'I use my wellies for gardening,' said Nellie Benson looking out suspiciously at the damp day. 'I have a pair of Dr Scholl's somewhere.'

Fanny said with fortitude that they would be better.

'Come in,' said Nelly.

'It's all right. We'll be in the car.' Mabel, who had dressed carefully in a powder blue suit and a hat of green-black feathers with a veil – bought once for the Queen's Birthday in Dar-es-Salaam – got quickly into her car and looked into the distance. Heaving the shopping bag ahead of her, Nelly climbed in alongside and said, 'I remember that hat. Always reminded me of a dead blackbird,' and laughed at this all the way along Kensington High Street.

Fanny said, 'I think perhaps we are out of the fourth form now, Nelly,' and Mabel did not speak.

'Where are you now?' Nelly asked when she had stopped laughing. 'What's become of you, Mabel? I heard you'd had to sell the castle.'

'Yes.'

'Suppose old Humphrey lost his money.'

'Oh Nelly, be quiet,' said Fanny in the back.

'Horses, I suppose. He always lost. I remember the Marsa Club in Malta. My word he flung it about. Where d'you live now?'

'Newbury.'

'Bit near the course, isn't it?'

'He watches on television,' said Mabel, negotiating the Kensington traffic lights with knuckles of ice.

'You can do that anywhere – watch the television. Unless you're like me – can't afford one. Where d'you live, Fanny?'

'Wimbledon.'

'Oh dear, that's a pity. A long way from London. Further than Newbury in a sense.' She began to laugh again.

'We're very comfortable.'

'Do be quiet, Nelly. Fanny lives in a charming house in Fethney Road. Delicious red brick. I wouldn't be surprised if it was Norman Shaw. I thought all your little things looked lovely there, Fanny.'

'Norman Shaw?' said Nelly, 'Wasn't he A. D. C. Pankot? Terrible old pansy. Dench couldn't bear him. Have you got any of *his* little things?'

'Oh for goodness sake!' said Fanny. 'Don't be so foul Nelly.

Mabel means the things we've all got – brasses and elephants' feet, the things we've all got and can't bear. I like Fethney Road. I don't know the locals but there's the Diplomatic Wives. I go to those in London.'

'Dench would have approved of that. Poor Dench, she was never a Diplomatic Wife. Or any wife at all. I wonder why?' said Mabel.

'We were always wondering why. So pretty she must have been. Men loved her.'

'Yes. I don't think they ever got very far with her though.'

'Not that she was a puritan – my word no. Just – withdrawn somehow. Deep down. Knew how to stop things going to far. My word she'd have a marvellous D. W. Complete gent of course.'

'Oh, complete.'

'And knew her place.'

'Oh yes, she knew her place.'

'There had been some man once, you know. D'you remember? The children used to tease her. Mr Santas-somethingorother. Some Argentine millionaire. Some Widower –'

'No. Not a widower. Very much married. Catholic. What was his name? The children used to call him Mr Salteena.'

'She didn't like jokes about him. D'you suppose he existed?'

'No idea. But it is funny she didn't marry. D'you think she was a Lesbian? A lot of nannies are. Subconsciously of course.' said worldly Mabel.

'Certainly not,' said Nelly, outraged. 'Dench a subconscious!'

'And she wasn't a nannie either,' said Fanny. 'She was a gent. She was a romantic.'

'She was damn useful,' said Nelly. She eased her legs out of the car and felt for Hans Crescent with the Dr Scholl's. 'We're lucky to find a parking place I suppose, but this is a good long way from Harrods.'

'We'll go in at door ten,' said Mabel. 'Past the children's hairdressing and the rocking horse. Then through the children's clothes to get to the lifts. In memory of Dench. She brought all my children here, Fanny, at one time or another.'

'She brought all mine,' said Fanny.

'I dare say she brought mine,' said Nelly, 'though I can't say I knew anything about it. I just handed the lot of them over to her. They were happier with her anyway. My place was with Charles.' She waddled ahead.

Hatted and handbagged, not to say shopping-bagged, talking in piercing, old-fashioned Kensington voices, the three old women watched children pitching on the rocking-horse, waiting for their hair to be cut. The ones with nannies all had dusky skins. The white ones were mostly with tired-looking mothers wearing anoraks and reading *Cosmopolitan*. The dusky ones wore herring-bone tweed, the white ones space-suits. White or dusky they all screamed a good deal.

'What would Dench have thought of this!' said Fanny.

'She'd have borne it. Perhaps improved things.'

'Oh, she'd not have gone to Arabs!'

'Oh I don't know. Look at Anna and the King of Siam.'

'Dench didn't care about money,' said Mabel. 'That was the really lovely thing about her.'

'Yes,' said Fanny, 'Dench was cheap.'

Up in the lift the ladies rose, to the fourth floor and the big airy restaurant where they had booked a table. The head-waiter on seeing Lady Benson's shoes found that the table was after all another table – one in a corner and rather behind a screen. Mabel's long finger summoning him back took a little time to be regarded.

'A young woman will be joining us. A Miss Dench.'

'Yes, madam.'

'Show her to this table, will you?'

'Yes, madam. Sherry, madam, while you are waiting?'

There was an uneasy, negative movement, a slight sliding away of eyes.

'Not yet, thank you.'

'How will we know her – the niece? She's quite young, isn't she?' said Fanny. 'She sounded quite young in the letter. I suppose she's a great-niece. How are we going to know her? I mean, any of these women might be nieces,' she looked about, 'eating their lunch.'

'Well, a lot of people are nieces. And eat lunch. We have been nieces –'

8

'Not primarily,' said Fanny. 'We were never primarily nieces. All these women look primarily nieces. It's very depressing. It's rather a test when you think about it – looking a niece. Dench herself for instance would never have looked a niece. Mr Salteena would never have fallen for a niece. We don't look nieces –'

'Don't know what you're talking about,' said Lady Benson, munching a roll.

'Well, I dare say we'll spot Niece Dench,' said Mabel. 'I believe I once saw her as a matter of fact. I went to East Molesey to see Denchie – oh, seven or eight years ago. She must have let me in. A nice little woman. I expect she'll come back to me. There was masses of ironing about.'

'Ironing?'

'Yes. On airers. You know those old-fashioned standing airers. All round the sitting-room. Beautiful ironing it was – I remembered the smell – lovely warm clean clothes, and Denchie in a bed in the corner. She did look small.'

'Yes. I think she must be a very good sort of woman, the niece.'

Fanny said uncertainly, 'I suppose that's what she meant about a nursing home,' but Mabel said, 'Oh, come on – Dench was no trouble. And she ate like a bird. Don't you remember in the War? If ever we got anything on the Black Market and there wasn't enough to go round Dench never minded being left out. There were some eggs once – it was when we were in Lincolnshire and she was cook-house-keeping – six beautiful eggs and we had them boiled for a treat. There were Humph and I and the children and some child staying – little Polly Knox. D'you remember? Pretty baby thing – Dench adored her. Seven of us and only six eggs and someone said, "What about Dench?" Polly Knox said, "You can have half mine, Denchie" – and Dench said straightaway, "Thank you, dear, but I don't take eggs." '

'She used to say that about cream in the War, "No thank you, I don't take cream. Not since Canada." '

'She'd been a hero in Canada, you know. Nursed a typhoid case nobody else would touch – and caught it and nearly died. She'd volunteered – it was in all the Canadian papers. It was while we were over there. She got flowers from all over the

9

place. Rather marvellous for her – except for being so delicate afterwards, no cream and so forth. Oh and having no money – otherwise she had a pretty good life I'd say, Denchie. I wonder if she had the OAP – I never paid her stamp, did you?'

'No.'

They fell silent. No niece appeared. The waiter drew closer holding pencil and pad.

'D'you think we should have sherry?' said Fanny.

'All right. All right, yes. She's very late. We'll have sherry. Three sherries please. Very dry and – well what about ordering some wine? I mean this is to be a tribute, isn't it – instead of the first idea of putting something in the paper. More lavish. And romantic. And very much nicer for us. I want to do it properly. I want the niece to feel we've done things properly. Do they have half bottles?'

'We can't order wine,' said Nelly, 'until we know what the niece is going to eat.'

The sherries came as they considered. Lady Benson decided she had lost her shopping-bag, then, finding it, wondered if she had time to go downstairs to the Food Halls for a pound of Finnan Haddock which though expensive was more certain than in Notting Hill not to be coloured cod.

Dissuaded by the others she sat on, and at last when the niece was more than half an hour late they ordered.

'It seems,' said Mabel to the waiter, 'that our friend is not coming. We will have three chicken a la king.'

'Anything to start with, madam?'

'No thank you.'

'Vegetables?'

'Er – perhaps a green salad.'

'I'd like vegetables,' said Lady Benson. 'I seldom seem to eat vegetables.' But a chill stare from Mabel sent him off.

'D'you remember the lovely vegetables in Hong Kong?' said Nelly. 'They used to fly the lettuces from America.'

'That was Jamaica.'

'Do you get vegetables, Fanny?'

Fanny said they had good Brussels sprouts.

'I don't see any point in spending money,' said Mabel, 'if the niece isn't here.'

'We were never *in* Jamaica,' Nelly said. 'Nor Africa. I'm glad to say we never had to go through Africa, Charles was always too senior.'

'I can't see how he can *always* have been too senior.'

'The place none of us ever got to,' said Mabel, 'senior or otherwise, was South America. D'you know that Dench knew South America? Very well. I first found her in Jamaica on her way back from Buenos Aires sitting all by herself at a table at The Mona – eating lettuce, I dare say. Perhaps Brussels sprouts. I thought, what a charming little woman and how sad she looks. I suppose she'd just left Salteena.

'So fragile. So sad. Not a bean. The children took to her and I thought well, she might be just the thing, and I took her on. And that was over forty years ago.'

'Devoted,' said Fanny. 'Utterly reliable.'

'More than the niece,' said Mabel. looking towards the door where a dazzling woman had just come in wearing a tightly-belted Persian lamb jacket with mink lapels. Her long legs wore long grey suede boots. Her coat and skirt said Paris. Not young, she made youth seem a triviality.

'Not,' said Mabel, 'that I ever felt we were real favourites with Dench!'

Fanny said, 'I thought you were. I never really felt we were. She talked of your children all the time.'

'To us she talked of yours.'

'She never talked to anyone about mine,' said Lady Benson, 'and neither did I.'

'Used to send her good presents though,' she added. 'Pound of tea at Christmas. When we were in Ceylon.'

'The child she really did love more than the rest was that child Polly Knox,' said Mabel, 'the one who tried to share the egg.'

'Yes, but then that *was* an easy child. My word she was a clever girl, too. She did do well for herself.'

'Yes – Charles and I paid to go over that place once. Chateau. They weren't there. Somewhere else in another chateau I dare say. Rolling. My dear, that woman is coming over to this table. You don't think it could be the niece?'

'Not if the niece is bringing presents. This one's not carrying presents.'

11

A uniformed chauffeur, however, walked behind with parcels and they both approached. The woman, who looked more beautiful as she came nearer, spread Persian-lambed arms and cried 'Dears!'

The three ladies sat like rocks.

'I'm so terribly sorry. We found it so difficult to park. Chetwode couldn't stay with the car because of the parcels. I'm so fearfully late. Oh I do hope you haven't waited. Oh good – you haven't. Thank you, Chetwode, just here on the window-sill. I'm afraid they're nothing. She said in the will you were to have mememtoes, but she had so little. You'd not believe how little. So few possessions. There – well –' She looked round. The chauffeur melted. Her hair was the colour of very pale sunshine, her eyes enormous, clear and contrite. She took off her gloves and revealed beautiful long-fingered hands which she first clasped and then undid and waved about.

'Champagne,' she cried. The head-waiter who had come close came closer. 'Champagne. We are here to celebrate,' she told him, 'the life, the *happy* life of the dearest, dearest old –. No I won't call this an In Memoriam. Denchie couldn't bear going on about the past. She had the happiest life and she died peacefully and thinking about us all. A good dry – yes that one. Number six.'

Mabel said faintly that she was very glad about Dench's happiness. Nelly Benson said nothing and Fanny Soane shut her eyes and opened them again.

The niece. The niece so good at ironing.

'I believe she talked of you three,' said the niece leaning forward, 'more than anyone else. Day after day, year in year out. All the places she had seen through you and how you rescued her, Mrs Ince, when she was in very low water and let her have an absolutely free hand with all your children – let her nurse them when they were ill. And even *grand*children, Lady Benson.'

Bewildered at being recognised and so warmly, and unable to keep her eyes off the niece's sapphire and diamond ring Mabel said stiffly, 'We grew to rely on her very much.' Lady Benson began to say that Dench knew her pl—, but stopped to watch the

12

niece's easy greeting of the champagne and the arrangements to make the bill for it separate and hers. Fanny watching the niece draw from her silky handbag a silky tenner said that all three had known Dench for a very great number of years. Probably better than anyone else. The quality of the niece's pale silk shirt made her flush suddenly with fury (By God, nursing homes!).

'Dench was an excellent servant,' she said.

The niece raised her glass. 'To Dench,' she said.

They drank.

'D'you remember *The Times*?' said the niece.

'Only just. We gave up our idea of that sort of tribute. *The Telegraph* is somewhat not –'

'No, no – I mean Dench and *The Times*? How she wrapped herself in *The Times* all the way from Perth when there was no room for her with you in the first class and there was no heating in those days in the thirds?'

'I don't think –' said Mabel.

'I never really believed in that frost-bite business,' said Fanny.

'Do you remember the roses?' said the niece.

Nobody remembered the roses.

'I think it was one of your daughters, Lady Benson, when Denchie had been looking after Simon and Sara and Simon kicked her. Your daughter said, "Denchie, you must have some roses" and took the secateurs and a basket and led her out into the gardens and cut three. Three roses – wasn't it priceless? D'you remember those gardens – there were two thousand rose trees. One of the sights of Persia. Oh how Denchie laughed!'

'I don't suppose,' said Nelly Benson, 'that Dench had much room for displaying roses.'

'Oh no. No, no of course not. She was in the attics. She wasn't minding. It just made us both laugh.'

'I felt personally very sorry,' said Mabel after a moment, 'about the business of the nursing home. I would have liked to help Dench, even taken her myself for a week or two, just to help the family out. But we were abroad.'

'Oh, but she refused. Didn't you know? You mustn't worry. It was all arranged for the nursing home without your kind help but she was so miserable. She said, "Oh do let me stay at home."

She liked being in the sitting room. So of course we let her. I promise you she never knew you had been asked.'

Lady Benson who had let the Dr Scholl's stray under the table tried to retrieve them and said, 'She always had my shoes. It's the thing I miss most if you want to know – good shoes.'

'The shoes are still there,' said the niece. 'Rows and rows. They are very old-fashioned but if you wished I could let you have them back I'm sure. Dear Denchie never wore them – they were too big, though she was a lamb and I'm sure she never told you.'

'And these,' she said stretching out to the window-sill (the waiters leapt) 'are the little mementoes – all I could find and I do feel so sorry, just little brass things, Benares trays, a hand bell, an elephant's foot – it could be adapted as a boot scraper.'

They held their gifts.

'It is very good of you to bother,' said Mabel at last, 'to bring them all this way.' The full horror of the presents had made her turn quite pink. Pink with triumph. She knew that had she discovered Dench to have had anything really –

'I feel very *honoured*,' she said. 'To think that this sort of thing was all she had. All Denchie had.'

'Well, except for the money,' said the niece.

'Money?'

'Yes. The South America money. Mr Salteena's money as we children used to call him.'

'Did he leave her –? You mean he did exist?'

'Oh yes. Mr Salteena existed. He left her four hundred.'

'Oh but how nice!'

'Thousand, that is. He left her four hundred thousand. She left two hundred thousand of it to me and the other two hundred thousand to her niece.'

'You,' said Lady Benson with a void and wallowing noise in the throat. 'You then are not the niece?'

'The niece! Darling, darling Lady Benson – didn't I say? Didn't you recognise me? Oh dear I thought you'd recognise me. I was fussed being late. Oh how silly! I forgot to say – the niece said no. She couldn't face it, she said, not Harrods. And – the money's not altered her a bit – she said she had the ironing.'

14

'But who then –?' said Mabel.

'Well, but I'm Polly Knox. You must remember me. I'm Polly Knox. I've never lost touch with Dench. She left me half and I've been astounded and quite speechless ever since. He only died a short time before she did, Mr Salteena, but she was absolutely in her right mind and all that when she heard. She quite understood. Her niece said she just lay there in bed with the solicitor's letter on the counterpane and she smiled. And she said – to the niece – the niece told me – she's very straight and she told me this – she said, "Why Polly Knox, Auntie?" and Denchie said and, well, we've all been wondering what on earth she meant, she said –'

'What did she say?' asked Mabel Ince with unmoving lips.

'Well, she said a funny thing. She said, "Tell Polly she shall have half my egg." '

15

Hetty Sleeping

Seeing the tall man's long back she thought with a lurch, 'It's like Heneker's back.' Then as he turned round she saw that it was Heneker.

He was standing on a pale strip of sand near the sea, looking down into the cold water, quiet as he had always been, peaceful, unmistakable.

'How *could* it be?' she thought. 'What nonsense! Of course it can't be.'

She went on folding the tee-shirts and jeans, gathering flung sandals, then made two neat heaps with a towel on each, for when the children came out of the sea. She took off her cardigan, pushed her hands back through her hair, gave her face for a moment to the sun; looked again.

She watched her two children run with drumming feet over the hard white strand, splash past the man into the sea, fling themselves in to it in fans of spray, shrieking. Then she looked at the man again.

Long brown legs, long brown back. He was watching with a painter's concentration the movement of the water and the shapes of the children playing in it. Twenty, thirty yards away, yet she could not mistake the slow smile, the acceptance as he narrowed his eyes and looked at lines and planes and shadows that there are wonders on the earth.

It was Heneker all right. Ten years older but decidedly and only Heneker.

He turned, came up the beach, dropped down beside her and said 'Hullo.' He was wearing black swimming trunks and had a beard. 'Funny,' she thought, 'I always laugh at beards in the sea, but he looks all right. He always did look alright. Wherever he was.'

'Hullo,' she said.

He hadn't said her name. Perhaps he'd forgotten it. He had never used people's names much. He had been cautious. Except in his work.

'Hullo, Hetty,' he said. 'It's a long time.'

'It's a funny place,' she said. He smiled, not looking away from her face. 'To meet again,' she said. 'It's a long way from Earl's Court. Connemara.'

'A holiday,' he said gently and began to take the sand and sift it through his fingers. Her heart started to lurch again seeing his fingers. 'I know each nail,' she thought, 'I know each line on them. Every half moon. Oh God!'

There was a shriek from the sea and he looked over his brown shoulder at the children. 'Yours?' he said.

'Yes.' She began to babble. 'They're eight and four. Andy and Sophie. We're here for a fortnight. We've taken a house.'

'And their Papa?'

'He's following. He was to have come with us but at the last minute there was a crisis. We came ahead. We'd booked the house you see. The Pin.'

'The Pin? Lord Thing's house? Ballinhead?'

'Yes. It's a fishing lodge –'

'I know.' He swung round on to his stomach and got hold of her bare feet and held them tight. 'Hetty,' he said, looking closely at her toes. 'Wonderful feet,' he said. 'They always were. I once drew your feet. So you've married brass?'

'No,' she said. 'When we married there was no brass at all. He's clever. He's good. At his job. Marvellous if you want to know.'

'Top brass?'

'Not at all. Don't be silly. I was a painter. Would I have married top brass?'

'Very silly not to if you had the chance. Colonel and Lady Top-Brass, V.C., X.Y.Z. and Bar. Are you Lady Brass? You look it a bit, with your white, white skin.'

'Don't be silly –'

He held her feet tight and put his forehead against them. 'Lord and Lady Top-Brass and all the little alloys.'

'Shut up!' (This can't be happening! We arrived yesterday.

17

We've hardly been here ten minutes! Heneker!) She tried to free her feet and giggled. 'You're tickling,' she said. 'Don't *breathe* over me.'

He let go her feet and said, 'What is he then?'

'A banker.'

'Christ!'

'Do you know any bankers? Men with international work?'

'No, thank God. "Men with international work." Do you know any painters still?'

'No,' she said.

'Do you do any painting?'

After a long time she said no.

He lay flat on his back now on the sand and spread his arms far out and closed his eyes. His bearded, gentle face and fine nose and peaceful expression were like an ikon. She thought, 'He ought to be picked out in jewels he's so beautiful. He's wicked as ever. Oh God, I love him,' and getting up she gathered the two heaps of clothes with a swoosh into the beach bag and the cardigan and her book and the towels in her arms, and was off down the beach to the sea's edge. 'I'm moving,' she called to the children. 'I'm going back up to the car. Don't be long, darlings. Ten minutes.'

'But we've just got *in*! We were staying in all morning.'

'There's a wind.'

'But it's *lovely*!'

'No, it's cold. I'm moving out of the wind.'

'There's not a breath of wind,' shouted Andy. 'Not a bit. You're crazy. It's a *boiling day*.'

'I'll be up in the car,' and resolutely, not looking back, she tramped up the beach alone and sat by the car in the sharp grass among old picnic papers, where red ants nipped her and noisy wild dogs from the fishermen's cabins came and barked endlessly for food as she pretended to read.

She was bathing Sophie at The Pin that evening in water that foamed like Guinness into the noble old Guinness-stained bath-tub when a noise of thundering hooves began to rock the bath-room ceiling and the water from the tap turned to a trickle and died.

18

'Now what!' Hetty sat back on her heels. 'Sixty pounds a week! Sixty pounds a week! The phone is dead, the electrics flicker and the beastly peat . . . And now *this*.'

'Whatever is it?' Andy came flying in.

'I don't know. I think it's the boiler or something. I think it's dry.'

'The water's hot as hot.'

'Yes, but it's stopped coming. The tank must be empty. It comes from that bog thing in the grounds – we saw it yesterday. I thought it looked awfully shallow.'

'It looked awfully dirty,' said Andy, 'and so does the bath.'

'No. It's lovely brown water,' she said. 'But, oh!'

'I expect it'll all blow up soon,' said Andy. 'Shall I go and throw the main switch? It might be safer.'

'No. Shush. Let me think.'

'Above the kitchen door. That great heavy big one?'

'No. Oh do shut up. Let me *think*. There's the pub. We might go to the pub. There might be a man.'

'There is a man.'

'At the pub?'

'No, here.'

'Here?'

'Yes. In the hall place. He's that man on the beach. He's playing with our plasticine. Wait, I'll ask him.'

Hetty on a cane chair by the bathroom window, with Sophie wrapped in a towel on her knee saw Andy and Heneker walking thoughtfully together, hand in hand through the wild garden towards the source of the bathwater.

The thunder in the roof, however, continued.

When she brought Sophie down the stairs Heneker was at the big trestle table in the hall making a plasticine dinosaur and without looking up said, 'There seemed nothing wrong down there. Must be a block in the pipe.'

She sat down with Sophie at the far end of the table and the booming grew less, then less still and finally stopped. A blessed trickle into the tank could be heard.

He said, 'Irish plumbing.' Sophie eating biscuits sidled round to him and watched his fingers and Andy who had been having his bath, which for safety's sake had been Sophie's not-run-out, came down again and leaned against Heneker

19

watching the emergence from the plasticine of a fat porcupine on elephant's legs, armour plated on the stomach and with a rhino's spike. Sophie coming closer gazed at it with love.

'Could I have it?' said Andy.

'Someone can,' said Heneker. He put it in the middle of the table with its nose in a bowl of fuchsias.

'Thirsty,' said Sophie. 'Poor pig.'

'It's not a pig. It's a – what is it, Heneker?'

'It's a swamp wanderer.'

'What's that?'

'It wanders through swamps. It squelches through bogs. It thunders in roofs –' They squealed with joy.

'Now then,' said Hetty, 'bedtime.'

Heneker made a roaring and thundering noise. They clung to him. '*Bed*time,' Hetty said, hearing her Surrey voice. 'Now that will do. You're over-excited. Go to bed.'

'Oh please –'

'No. If Daddy were here –'

'He's not. Can't we stay?'

'Off,' said Heneker. 'Quick before the squelcher gets you.'

They fled, Sophie stopping on the bend in the stairs, minute, delectable in a flowery nightgown. 'You won't go away? You'll come back tomorrow?'

'Yes,' said Heneker.

She brought coffee to the sitting-room where he was sitting in one of the two comfortable, shabby armchairs and watching the crumbling peat fire. Four long windows lit the chintz sofa, the shelves of Lord Thing's books about fishing and birds. Outside shone the Irish night, black and silver, with long bumpy spars of land running out towards America. Not a sound anywhere, never a light moving along the road. There was the sense that all about the holiday house lay miles of silence, darkness, the ancient mountains inland making a long barricade against the usual world.

Heneker's face as he sat far back in his chair was in shadow. She put the coffee between them on a stool and leaned back in her chair, too. They did not speak for a long time.

'It might have been like this,' he said at last. She felt her heart begin to thump and hung on to the chair. (This is *Heneker*.

20

Heneker I have thought of every day.)

'No,' she said.

He said, 'Yes. Oh God!'

'You never asked me,' she said, 'Not once.'

'Well you know why.'

'I don't know why.'

'Oh Hetty –'

'I don't know why. I never knew why. I couldn't ask you. All that year. That room . . . The bed made out of ropes. The roof like a greenhouse and the curtain over the corner.'

'Where our clothes were.'

'No. Our clothes were in heaps. Well your clothes were in heaps.'

'I loved your clothes.' he said. 'Always clean and neat. And small. All the buttons were real buttons with proper button-holes.'

'I used to gather up yours,' she said. 'Like gleaning. A sock here. A shirt there, a shoe on the light.'

'On the *light*?'

'Yes. To dim it down. Very dangerous.'

'And smelly.'

She laughed.

'Oh go on,' he said.

'What?'

'Laughing,' he said. 'I'd forgotten.'

'And now you're famous,' she said, looking up at him. He had stood up, all the long length of him, resting his forehead against his arm on the high chimneypiece and looking down at the grey fire. 'Heneker Mann.'

' "What a piece of work is Mann." Have you –?'

'Yes. I've been to all of them.'

'Exhibitions,' he said. 'God knows what they amount to really. I was doing better stuff that year.'

'No,' she said. 'You are very much better now.' (He still says things in order to be contradicted. He knows I will contradict. He knows that I know that he needs to be contradicted. Our thoughts move completely together. They always did. We sit here. We are like Darby and Joan . . . And it's ten years. He's wicked still of course. I suppose he's married, I wonder –')

'She's a painter,' he said to the fire.

Hetty said nothing.

'She's a painter, Lady Top-Brass, just a painter.'

'Well I suppose so. She would have had to be.'

'No. You know that. All that year you knew.'

'I didn't. Anyway, *I* was a painter.'

'No. You picked up my clothes. Took the shoe off the light.'

'Good painters are often tidy. Usually in fact. You must have been reading novels about painters, Heneker.'

'No,' he said. 'Not tidy like you. The tidiness was growing. It was getting dangerous. It got in the way.'

'Not often,' she said. 'As time went on you weren't there to see. I tidied round nothing and nobody. You were always out. Later and later. More and more.'

'You should have painted instead. If you'd painted then, instead of minding and tidying –' he flung away and looked out of a window at the gigantic sea. 'God, I missed you.'

One of the children called out upstairs and in a second she was out of her chair and the room and gone. Sophie lay like a seraph, her face lifted to the moonlight but Andy was flinging about in a heap, one arm flailing the air. 'A spike,' he cried. 'Kill it.'

'All right,' she said, 'Hush. Wake up a minute.'

'Beast,' he cried. 'Thump it.'

'It's just a dream,' she said. 'You're asleep. You're sleeping – remembering the water tank.'

'Huh!' he said and, turning into a hump, was asleep again. She stood looking at herself in the glass at the top of the stairs, put back a strand of hair. 'Thirty-one,' she thought. 'Honestly, you wouldn't think so.' She felt gloriously happy, drifted back to the sitting-room. But Heneker was gone.

'After all, it was you left me,' he said.

'No.' She folded clothes. The children splashed, called, 'Heneker! Come and look. *Crabs*, Heneker!'

'Soon,' he said. He sat on a rock with a towel round his neck. She sat a little below him on the sand, his bare brown leg from knee to ankle beside her shoulder as she pushed Andy's socks into sandals. It was next day, still boiling, still un-Irishly hot.

'Your parting,' he said, 'is very beautiful.'

' "Was", I suppose.'

'No. Is. Your parting now, I mean. In your hair. All the hairs are bending back and shining down each side.'

'Oh, Heneker.' (Why is it that when he decides not to touch you it's as good as other men touching you? Better.) 'I thought you never liked my hair.'

'I never said that. Just thought it was – too symmetrical in those days. Over-nice. Better now.'

'I wasn't over-nice in the end.'

'Indeed no,' said Heneker. 'It was you left me, as I remarked.'

He slid down off the rock and sat beside her. 'And got married,' he said, leaning the back of his head against the rock he had been sitting on, 'about ten minutes later. God knows all about it I suppose. I didn't. The boy next door. Number three in *The Times*. Wedding in Scautland among all the dowdy dowagers. To which I was not invited.'

'Hardly.'

'Incidentally, is dowager a derivative? Of dowdy? One should look it up. Will you be a dowager? I'll marry you.'

'You're being cruel.' She began to get up.

'STOP!'

The long brown hand, ten years older but as familiar as her own, at last fastened over hers. 'Stop. Don't go.'

'Why the hell shouldn't I?'

'Don't go. With your white, white skin.'

'If I'm dowdy –'

'Oh, Het. Shut up.'

They sat on the almost empty strand. Some Dubliners far across were assembling a boat. There were one or two other people. Two fishermen trudged up from the day's work carrying a plastic bag with heavy fish in it staining the bag with blood. They were dressed in ageless clothes. They had very ancient faces. But for the plastic bag they might have been ghosts. They walked up past Sophie and Andy who were digging a fortress, Sophie patting the top of a Norman keep with a little pink spade. Her forearms were gold.

' 'Tis a beautiful day,' said the older fisherman as they passed by. 'You have beautiful children.' The younger fisherman looked at Hetty. They went on up the beach.

'I love you so,' said Heneker.

She pulled hard against his tightening hand.

'So what did you do?' she asked in the end.

He was leaning back still with eyes closed.

'Got married I suppose.'

'Suppose? You must know. To the one who – to the one you were –'

'No,' he said, sitting up. 'Not her.'

'Well, to a painter.'

'Yes. To a bloody good painter if it is of any interest to you.'

Andy came up and flung down crabs. Sophie fell on a squishy thing and cried. Comfort. Handkerchieves. Clothes. Home for lunch and the children's rest; Heneker back to the pub where he was staying.

'Will you come up after and do plasticine beasts, Heneker?'

'Yes, all right, Andy. Half past seven.'

'I was supposed to be a bloody good painter too.' She put down the coffee tray again between them, tried to brighten the fire, opened the curtains wider to the evening sea. 'Until I met you.'

'That's what I mean.'

'You destroyed it.' She poured the coffee into mugs. 'That's all. Anyway you were no good to me. You're no good to any woman.'

'Any brown sugar?' he said.

'No.'

'I'd have thought that Lord Thing kept brown sugar for his coffee, Lady Top-Brass. Lady Brass-Tops.'

'The groceries aren't in with the rent. They're provided by me. Well, by Charles. You can't get demerara in the village –' she had to stop.

'Darling,' he said, coming over and taking her hands. 'Darling, for God's sake, don't. Don't cry. Whatever –'

'You're so bloody cruel. You always were so bloody cruel.'

'But truthful,' he said squeezing her hands so that they hurt. 'Always that. And to no one else. Not truthful like this.'

'Thank you very much.'

'Oh, Het. Don't be cruel back. God, you were always crueller. You know you were, too. You could get in where it hurt. Because you knew –. Where're you going?'

He caught up with her as she reached the hall, at the foot of the stairs beside the telephone which stood in the curl of the banisters – an old-fashioned telephone with a trumpet and a very old wire drooping out of it like a brown string chain. 'Het,' he said, grabbing her. The telephone tottered and he caught it and, 'Marvellous!' he said, looking at the telephone. 'God, it's nice. Like a black daffodil. Does it work?'

She flung off up the stairs leaving him with the telephone next to his heart. 'I'll go back to the pub then.' She answered by closing her bedroom door and heard him walk slowly down the weedy drive between the giant rhubarb, the wilderness of fuchsias, to the great, crumbling gate-posts. Once, twice she heard him stop. Savagely, delightedly, she imagined him looking back at the house all in darkness, her bedroom window dark as all the rest.

'Don't move.'

She put an arm across her forehead and looked out under it. He was drawing. 'Shut your eyes again. Put your arm down, Het.'

After a time she said, 'Can I open them now? I want to see if the children –. I fell asleep.'

'They're all right,' he said. 'I can see them. They're shrimping in a pool. I've been drawing them, too.'

'However long have you been here?'

'About an hour. You were deep asleep. With the red ants walking all over you.'

'I don't believe that.'

'The fishermen had a good look, too.'

'I didn't sleep much last night.'

'You went to bed too soon, Hetty of the white, white skin. Here you are, you never were one to get sunburned.' He threw the drawing across to her. 'Hetty Sleeping.'

'It's – lovely.'

'And here's the children.' Sophie's round, firm cheek, a sweep of eye-lash, her wrist still with its foetal crease over the wrist top.

25

Andy's long head, clear eyes; another drawing of his head from behind, the heart-breaking tail of hair (left from baby-hood) lying in the dent down the back of the neck.

'Have you any children, Heneker?'

'No.'

He got up and loped towards the sea and Sophie and Andy seeing him nearby sprang up to follow. She saw Andy show him something from a pool, Sophie lift her arms to be picked up. Heneker, examining in one hand the object from the pool, swung Sophie up with his other arm onto his shoulder and the three of them stood reflectively together, illuminated, at peace.

'Tomorrow,' said Heneker, eating her sandwiches at lunch-time – it was too beautiful a day to go back to the house, too good for the children to waste in resting – 'tomorrow we'll go to the Clifden Show and see the ponies. We'll go on the bus.'

'Whyever the bus?' she said.

'To see some people.'

'Will you draw the people on the bus?' asked Andy.

'I might.'

But he didn't.

They sat in a row on either side of the gangway, Hetty with Andy, Heneker with Sophie who soon got on his knee, and listened to the talk around them and watched the sea and the bog and the procession of the Connemara mountains, purple and graceful behind the orange gorse and the great scattering of white stones. At Clifden they walked the fair and touched the ponies and brought things and ate things and drank things and lived in the lovely crowd. Heneker in washed-out blue denim, brown-faced, lanky as a cowboy with the two small children trotting behind him, turned heads. Hetty carrying the picnic in a big, round basket she had found among the fishing tackle in the house, in sandals and a handkerchief over her head and a faded red dress bought years ago in Florence, walked easily along feeling she might be taken for a tinker. Happy and weary at five o'clock they caught the bus home, Sophie falling deep asleep in Heneker's arms, Andy moving over beside him. Hetty set the basket on the seat left empty beside her, and, like a peasant, shielded her eyes from the levelling sun.

Back at Heneker's pub where the bus stopped he lifted Sophie carefully down and put her in the back seat of Hetty's car. Andy stumbled in beside her, then stuck out his head.

'You coming back too, Heneker?'

'No. It's supper-time at the pub.'

'Mummy could cook you some with us.'

'No, they'd be cross at the pub if I didn't turn up. It'll be ready.'

'Why would they? You could still pay. Why don't you come and stay with us? There's heaps of room. You could sleep next to Mummy.'

His clear voice carried across the pub yard and some people coming up from the beach looked amusedly at them, and a girl – the waitress or barmaid who had been leaning against the bar door – disappeared, slamming it behind her.

'I can't do that.' Heneker flicked Andy's nose. 'But you must go. It's been a long day.'

Hetty started the car. He came round to her side of it and said, 'I'll walk over later.'

It was a question made to sound like a statement. Not looking at him but busily at the gears she said, 'All right,' and swung through the gate and up the hill.

When the children were fed and in bed, drugged and rosy with sun, she bathed and changed, trying on first one thing and then another, ending up with a long cotton dressing-gown. She put up her hair on top of her head where it immediately began to fall down. Rather successfully. She took off her shoes and wandered to the kitchen to find something for supper, but nothing seemed to make her feel hungry. She ate a tomato by the fridge, staring through the kitchen window at the high, neglected grass and the tall Evening Primroses that slapped the pane. She laid the coffee tray.

Then she walked to the sitting-room and struggled half-heartedly with the faint fire. The sun, now setting in a blaze beyond the point, turned the room to glory, lighting up a filmy silvery peaty dust on the old furniture, making a great vase of flowers and leaves she had gathered yesterday glow rose red. 'It's like a dream,' she thought. She walked all round the house and

27

then into the garden, pacing its boundaries on her bare feet, discovering an overgrown fishpond, peering into long-empty stables with trees growing through the roofs, disturbing three lean sheep from under an old mounting-block. She walked the long way back to the front door and stood a while looking out to sea and determinedly not towards the road.

Then she went in and lit the kettle. Then she turned it off. She went up to look at the children and coming down again looked at last unashamedly down the long, empty drive. She went back to the sitting-room and sat in the arm chair and looked at the black turf on the fire. The sun had quite gone and the room was cold. It was half past ten.

He was not coming.

As she fell asleep she saw a sudden image of Charles's alert and prudent face. She thought, 'Charles always saw me right home to the door.'

'Hetty sleeping.'

She jumped with such a jerk she felt quite sick, and sat bolt upright. Heneker was opposite her in the other chair. He was laughing. 'Hetty very deeply sleeping.'

'Where were you? Where am I?' she cried. 'Heneker – it's midnight. Where've you been?' It was ten years ago. But where was the glass roof, the smell of Earl's Court? 'Where've you been. I've been all alone.' She looked around. It was now. Ireland. The expensive, rented house. Children. Charles somewhere in the world. Charles –.

'The children,' she said, 'I must see if the children are all right. The doors are all open. Anyone could have walked in.'

'It was I walked in.'

'But anyone could have. The I.R.A. –'

'Don't be silly, Het.'

'You had no *right* to walk in.'

'You said I was to come.'

'But it's the middle of the night.'

'I was held up. It's a long walk here.'

'You've never been as late as this.' She heard the voice, high, accusing. Oh God! Like a wife. Like then. It's no different.

Wearily she got up. 'I must go and look at the children, Heneker,' and walked slowly away.

But on the stairs she stopped and after a while gave a sigh and turned and sat down, resting her head against the banisters. All the doors were open in the hall, and through the open front door on the right the moonlight flooded in, and the heavy, dementing scent of the night flowers in the garden. She shut her eyes.

'Het,' he was at the foot of the stairs beside the ancient telephone. 'Het,' he lifted his arm. 'Oh, my dear Het.'

She pulled herself up and helplessly walked down back to him until she was two steps above him, level with his eyes.

'Sleep with me, Hetty,' he said and she said, 'Of course.'

Between them on the banister the telephone began to ring.

'It can't! It doesn't!'

'Well, it is.'

'It can't. It never has. It's terrible.' She covered up her ears.

'You'd better answer it.'

'I can't. I can't,' she cried.

'Well I can't, can I? For God's sake, stop the bloody thing.' He walked over to the open front door.

Looking at him all the time she picked up the heavy ear-piece and heard a tremendous crackling, then the voice of a sleepy post-mistress, more crackling and then from some ethereal wasteland, Charles.

'Hester? Hester? Where on earth? God-forsaken –'

'Here I am,' she said, 'Yes? Charles?'

'. . . coming at once.'

'You're coming when?'

'I'll be there . . . ,' more huge crackling, '. . . over at last.'

'I didn't hear. When? Where are you? *When* are you coming?' The crackling grew and became a pain in the ears, then stopped. There was silence.

'He's –. He's –. Charles. He's on his way.'

'Where is he?'

'I don't know. Perhaps in Clifden.'

'At twelve o'clock at night? Well, he'd not get here till tomorrow if he's off a bus.'

'Perhaps he's even at Ballynish.'

'Don't be silly. Why bother to ring if he were already at

29

Ballynish? He's probably still in Dublin. Or more likely still in London. Ringing from the Hilton. Carousing with the clients.'

'No. No. You don't understand Charles. I'm sure he's almost here.'

He grabbed the phone and threw it on the ground and took her wrists and said, 'Look. Sleep with me.'

'I can't. I can't.'

'All right.' He walked back to the door. She watched him turn back to her. Behind his head was the dazzle of the sea. 'There never was anyone but you, Het,' he said, and was gone.

'HESTER!' Charles's pleasant voice in the hall. Sounds of dropped luggage, Irish voices from the taxi. Half the village in attendance, much information being simultaneously imparted. 'What a journey! What a place to get to.' Shrieks from Sophie and Andy. 'Daddy! Oh – fishing rods! Did you remember to bring my orange bag? There are crabs, huge ones. Lobsters. We went to the fair.'

She watched them from the stairs, fickle, leaping like puppies, the taxi man, the taxi-man's assistant, the taxi-man's grandfather brooding by.

'Hester. Thank God. Damn thing over. Come and give us a kiss.' The attendants were paid off.

'How are you, love? Can't see you. Aren't there any lights? What's that thundering noise? Good heavens, what a telephone. Did I manage to get through on that?'

'The lights come and go,' she said. 'The thundering does too.'

'I'll fix it,' he said. 'The electrics will be the generator. I'll get on with it in a minute. It's very cold here.'

'We can't light the peat.' said Andy.

'But peat's marvellous, you useless creatures. I'll make a blaze. Where's the sitting-room? Better turn off the stop cock for the present. We're going out to supper.'

'We can't, there's only the pub. You have to book.' (What's the matter with my voice?)

'I've booked.'

'But the places round here don't – Hardly ever,' she said.

'I stopped at the pub on the way. Went in and booked. Come on. Get the children out of their night shirts, we're away to eat lobsters.'

'Charles – I can't go to the pub. I'm a mess. I'm tired. I waited all last night. We've waited around all today. It's after eight o'clock.'

'All last *night*? You didn't expect me last night? I didn't ring till midnight. I was still in London.'

'And by the way, something else,' he said as he drove them all fast down the hill. 'The Bartletts are at the pub.'

'The Bartletts? From home? From Denham Place? Oh no!'

'Yes – Have you got a sore throat? Said they saw you yesterday. With some splendid man.'

'I didn't see them.'

'I did,' said Andy. 'When we dropped Heneker at the pub.'

'Children are so odd,' she said to Cathie Bartlett in the pub. 'Andy saw you yesterday but he never said.'

'You seemed in a bit of a trance.' Cathie Bartlett's eyes were careful. Charles's great laugh rang out at something Bartlett had said. They were alone in the pub dining-room. A Bartlett child had come in from the television room and been gathered onto it's mother's knee. (But every knee is his knee. Every child is his child. Oh Heneker. Oh Heneker.)

'Famous chap,' said Bartlett. 'The great artist. Caused a stir.'

'Oh Heneker *Mann*,' said Charles. 'Oh, that's it. Old flame of Hester's, hey?'

'Yes,' said Hester. (I feel so far away.) 'I was a student of his at the Slade. Oh, donkey's years ago.' (Oh what can I do?)

'He's gone?' asked Charles.

'Gone all right. Disappeared this morning. Barmaid's gone too, I believe. There's a great to-do. Well – he'd been with her every blessed night.'

'Oh Noel!' said Cathie.

'Well he had. Be your age. These passages creak. We've not had a wink of sleep, Cathie and I, all week.'

'Don't blame her anyway,' said Cathie. 'Gorgeous. Don't mind telling you, Hester' – she lit a cigarette expertly above her child's head –, 'I was green with envy when I saw you with him on the beach. You ought to watch out, Charles.'

'Don't you worry,' said Charles.

They got up to go.

In Lord Thing's sitting-room the peat fire shone hot and

bright. Charles brought in the tray and put it on the stool, then drew the curtains. He said, 'I've settled the children. And I've had to make tea. I couldn't find any brown sugar.'

'I forgot it.'

'Never mind. Tea won't keep us awake. I say, what's this? "Hetty Sleeping".'

'Give me that.'

'No. Let me look. It's lovely. Wonderful.'

'It's mine. Charles – give it me. Give it me. *Give* it me.'

'No,' he said. He held the drawing at a distance under the brilliant electric light. ' "Hetty Sleeping".' He put on his glasses.

'Give me that. Give me that. Give me that!'

' "Hetty Sleeping",' he said. 'Very sadly.'

He put the drawing delicately down on Lord Thing's writing desk. Pouring tea for her he said, 'Sweet Hetty, wake up soon.'

Transit Passengers

'So, if it goes, it goes?'

'Yes.'

The rare bus was coming, ramshackle, in a cloud of dust, bright blue against the blocks of rock and blocks of small white houses. A man on a tall mule drew in to the side of the preposterous road. He was regal, with a hero's moustache, and did not turn to see whether his wife who walked behind, a witch bent over a long stick, or the white silk goat who walked behind her, would be able to draw in, too. The bus passed in a brown cloud and stopped by the sea-shore car park where the three students waited.

'It's here,' called the tall fair boy.

The dark girl got into the bus.

'Come on,' called the tall boy to the other one – a small American, bearded, bespectacled, reading a book, detached as a mole. In the bus all three had to sit separately in odd seats among the peasants, some with loaves and some with hens, and the tourists in their silver earrings bought in Ayios Nikólaos, with their sun-tans and guide books, who had come out here to see the hippies. The girl, big, with a wide shield of a face and a long dress made out of red- and grey-striped rough cotton, sat staring in front of her. Her eyes were dark and wide – very bright. She sat with knees apart under her long dress, easy, her arm touching the arm of the old man next to her but not noticing. The tall boy thought, she breathes out peace. Her luggage which neither of the boys had helped her with was on her knees in a canvas sack. From each side of her head above her ears scraps of hair coiled and twisted. They must have tickled her cheeks but she held the sack and did not tuck them away. Her legs were bare. She wore open-toed sandals dried and hard

33

as old seaweed. The tall boy had bare feet. The mole wore jeans, striped ankle socks and some leather shoes his grandmother had sent him from New York. Mark, the tall one, and the girl, Cassy, stared ahead, bumping and thumping and rocketing about the bus. The mole read.

They could not sit together in the plane either. It was a student charter flight and packed. Some were drunk and some were drunk with sun. Some were noisy and some complained of the service. At Athens they poured out and streamed with plastic parcels and bottles and string bags over the tarmac to the main building.

'Your plane's in half an hour,' said Mark to Cassy.

Cassy shifted her pack from hand to hand. They stood together in the place kept for transit passengers. 'I can never remember what it means,' said Cassy looking out at the Greek ...ountains, scalloped and pink, so different from the crags of Crete. '"Transit passengers". We all are.'

'Not if we've arrived.'

'Who's arrived?'

'Well – if you're stopping. Not going on.'

'It's not possible though, is it?' She speaks so slowly, he thought, she sometimes sounds almost stupid. For three months he had lived with her inside a Cretan mountain: on a shelf, in a fault in the shale, like swallows under a barn roof, except that the faults, the nests, were one beneath another down the rock, envelopes, like mille-feuilles. In each lifted envelope of rock the hippies lived, making a cave for themselves with some sort of a bed. Some hung a curtain or made a screen of branches, bought a gaz to cook with and a pan. They had a bad name. It said in the guide books that they begged in the villages and that the Cretans who had been used to giving hospitality since the days of Minos were now beginning to wonder why. The villagers watched the hippies – even now not knowing what hippies were – how they slept in the eaves of the mountain looking down at the clean, gritty beach where the clean green waves reared and crashed and sucked, publicly sleeping up there at odd hours, coming down late in the night to play music on guitars and lie about the sand drinking Pepsis out of tins. They were quiet enough people. The Cretan villagers were quiet, too, but bewildered by the openness of the young lovers. For they all were lovers. They all loved each other. They seemed half asleep and played poor music and draggled in long clothes, did without shoes and never went near the church and spent their time washing, washing, washing their bodies and their clothing and sucking at the sweet cigarettes. They never fought or were jealous or worked. Money now and then came out of the plastic folders – you took them to Heraklion and signed your name and came back on the bus with a wad of drachs. But they loved one another, the Cretans wonderingly acknowledged, watching the lanky English and Americans and big-boned Scandinavians sitting together in clusters or lying in each other's arms in the swallows' nests above the crashing sea. More like sleeping than loving, the Cretans thought. More like dying than sleeping.

'So, if it goes, it goes?' he said. 'You're sure?'

She was going back to London now – non-stop Heathrow 12.30 hours. Tunbridge Wells by midnight. The mole would be with her till Heathrow where he would consider. It would be New York then or New York later. Because of his grandmother (Monty – the mole – was a New Yorker who never spoke: a phenomenon). He had a First at Cambridge and a scholarship to take up either at Yale or Johns Hopkins. He was looking after Cassy for Mark till Heathrow.

'Look after Cassy,' said Mark, tall as a giraffe among the running Greeks, bright as Achilles, wretched as Achilles. 'Hey Monty, look after Cassy.' Monty put away the book on revolutions. He came just about to Cassy's shoulder. She was a tall girl and moved slowly. Her eyes at present were bright and not quiet.

'Cassy looks after me,' he said. 'She –'

'Cassy,' Mark said, 'you're sure I'm to go?'

They had slept together and lazed together from July to the end of September and he was going East for a year to his father who was a Hong Kong solicitor, she West, home to Kent, then to Cambridge. It was the time they call the best time of your life between school and university. They were both nineteen. The mole, already through with Cambridge and, so he said, with

35

most things, was twenty-three. He sat apart with his back to them and got the history book out again. Above their head a Greek voice began to cry out in a frenzy over a loud-speaker. Round them people started running.

'It's your plane,' he said, 'I think.'

'Yes,' she said. 'I want *The Guardian*.'

'It may not be yours.'

'Yes, it is. It's 603. I've learned some Greek. Thanks, Mont.'

'Some Cretan,' said Mark.

'Not much. I've not learned much. Not much more than before.'

'Look,' he said, 'I can still come back. Now. I don't have to go to my bloody father. I don't want filthy Hong Kong. It's just there's nowhere –'

'You've not seen him for two years.'

'His fault. He's got the money. He's a bloody rich lawyer.'

'No.'

'He's thick.'

'You don't know him, Mark.'

'He plays golf all the time.'

'Mark – you might get to China. That's why –'

'Yes,' he said, with such a knell of woe she laughed, and her large face grew alive and joyous. 'Oh Mark! China!'

'I don't want China. I want you. I can't do without you, Cassy, now.'

They stood together as the crowds went by and the Greek voice in the metal box yelled above them. 'It's been three months, Cassy.'

'Nothing.'

'I'll come back. In the spring I expect. I'll write every few days.'

'No.'

'I have to. I'll have no one to talk to. This thing – us – I think . . .'

'What?' She was almost alight with laughter beneath the skin, her eyes almost tearful, watching such a comedy.

'I think it's going to last with us,' he said, 'a long time.'

'What – through Hong Kong and Cambridge?'

'Yes. It won't stop. For me it won't stop.'

36

The mole pocketed the revolutions and took a can of Coke from his pocket. 'When you gotta go you gotta go,' he remarked, taking a swig. The announcer was becoming almost hysterical with anxiety. From the midst of the frantic chatter of starling Greek even names could now be distinguished. 'Miss Casseee Veeessee, Miss Cassseee Veeeeseeee, Mr Monty Fogelburg, Mr Monteee Fogel –'

'If it goes,' she said, coming across to Mark slowly in her long dress and putting down her sack which Monty gathered up. 'If it goes –'

'C'mon, Cassy,' Monty said, chucking the can in a bin. He had spoken thrice. It was an emergency. 'C'mon, Cass.'

'If it goes,' she said calmly, putting both arms round Mark's neck high above her and laying her head against the rough queer Arab robe she had made for him out of some stuff from Marshall and Snelgrove – 'If it goes, then of course it goes.'

He clutched her and said, 'It – I can't it won't stop. This is for a long time.'

But she released herself and they were gone through the barrier towards their plane. Monty turned as they reached the farther check-in where they began to be searched in the familiar way for drugs and bombs – passport pictures carefully checked against faces, luggage scattered, picked over by people, who should never never see it – should never see Cassy's most secret possessions which were so few and spare and good because she believed only in beauty and transience and the giving away of as much as possible and in no ties. Mark knew everything in Cassy's sack – some cotton shirts, a long cotton skirt, pants, a jersey for a cold day, a comb, soap, shampoo, *The Prophet* by Kahil Gibran which Monty laughed at, and a picture of her little sister. At first there had been a photograph of a heavy, jowled man and a woman beginning to go at the neck with a troubled face and pearl earrings, but these had gone. There were a dozen lemons, a bottle of honey and a postcard he had given her of the Minoan girl dug up at Knossos, the girl with the ringlets and the reckless mouth. He had written on the back, 'This is Cassy'.

He waited for them to be given back their belongings at the farther gate – his plane for Beirut, Bangkok, Hong Kong was not for ages. He waited for them to be signed off and hustled towards England and to turn and wave. He could still just see them at the end of the transit section, but the Greek police were taking their time with Monty. Beards mean pot. Thin American students with beards who do not speak and carry books on revolutions could mean heroin. Neither Cassy nor Mark nor Monty used anything, not even alcohol, not even meat, but always waited patiently through these formalities, indeed would have been insulted had they been considered unworthy of them. Monty was putting all the things back in his bag slowly and neatly. Cassy's beautiful broad back and long trail of hair could be seen beside him. Now they were through. She would turn.

But she did not. The two of them spoke briefly together and nodded. They each picked up their luggage and hurried off without looking back.

'She's gone,' he thought. 'She's not with me any more.'

His plane swooped up off the airport and swept like a swallow above the pink mountains. In a moment the airport was gone, only the fluted mountains lay bright in the evening light shadowed like upturned patty tins, the sea ridiculously blue, ridiculously white-fringed and postcard-like beside them.

Her plane was far away now. Above Italy now, over Rome. Or Florence. She's pointing out the Duomo, the Po valley. The Alps are coming up, have passed – the dull green plains and parquet fields of France. Tonight the standard roses on the lawn, lattice windows, the spaniel, roast chicken. 'Oh darling, it's lovely to have you back. Oh, such a long time. Plenty of hot water. How was Mark? And Monty? Such a character!'

Oh, I want you Cassy, Cassy.

Oh, I want you in our cave.

She's going up the stairs now in the red dress. ('Darling – that dress! Do you never wear anything else? However long since it was washed? There are three kittens. Hurry down.') She walks heavily and looks down from the half landing – still face, watchful eyes. Oh, Cassy, you never say a word you do not mean. Oh, Cassy, you are all hard sense. 'All right, Mark, it's love if you like. But if it goes, it goes.'

'But you see what I mean, Cassy? It's a test. If it lasts now – I love you, naturally.'

'Naturally?'

'Don't laugh. I don't see why I shouldn't say love. I do love you, Cassy. But if I come back to England now – Well I'll be back anyway next year –

'What I'm saying Cassy is, if it's going to be a – well, last a long time, well then, it'll last a long time. Won't it?'

'But if it's going to go,' she said, calm as a Greek sea under the moon, 'then it will go.'

They were dirty Arabs at Beirut with skeins of black wool round their heads. Air-hostesses – all knife-pleats and paint and hair-lacquer – pranced about, directing them with distaste. Australians drank out of bottles and shouted. The lights of Beirut twinkled in an arc around the great bay, higher and higher about the hills. Mark lay with his head on his pack and his eyes shut in the big dark lounge. The 747 was going to be late. Work out the time for Cassy. Long past midnight, nearly morning, she sleeping, her window shut against the cold after Crete; outside it, all the apples of Kent hanging away and away like round gold jewels decorating the Weald. Her bed will have clean sheets, the old dress dropped on the floor in a heap. She might be in a nightdress. Cassy in clothes in bed! Under his yellow beard he smiled.

'Flight to Bangkok,' the stewardess said sharply at his shoulder. 'Quickly.'

They sat in a block. An old American of tremendous size beside him asked for whisky. 'I wanna *bottle* of whisky,' he said. 'Yeah. And I want it now. A bottle. Right. And now bring me a glass.' He poured a paper carton the stewardess brought full of whisky to the brim and swilled it down as the plane took off. He held the bottle in one hand and the carton in the other, not being allowed to use his tray in case the plane crashed and it sliced him in half. 'I start with whisky,' he said to Mark. 'I always gotta be drunk before I can go down to Singapore.' He pronounced it 'Singapore'.

'It's Hong Kong,' said Mark, alarmed, 'isn't it?'

'That's right. Hong Kong.'

He began to pour a second carton and wag his head. A

Chinese sitting near moved no muscle. The pupil and the iris of their eyes are one, Mark thought.

'Ya hippy then?' asked the American. 'Jesus people? Can't give you any of this then. You'll be on the other stuff.' Without one hint of movement from muscle, nerve or bone Mark felt the disgust of the Chinese for the American. His interest stirred.

'Like this gang here,' said the fat man pointing at the Chinese and now very drunk. 'Keep it in the heels of their shoes. Any rate, you can't do that.' He wheezed with laughter and pushed a foot towards Mark's bare feet. Mark shrank and catching the Chinese's eyes felt sympathy. He nodded at him and the Chinese bowed gravely back. Only when the lights of the plane went out and the American slept did he put on the British Airways blue socks and then very surreptitiously and only because it was cold.

She'll be in bed for breakfast. She'll have the dog on the bed. There'll be toast and stuff – marmalade. The telephone'll be going. 'Is Cassy back?' She won't be caring – dump the tray on the floor, turn over, sleep, sleep. Such a heavy sleeper. Says so little. She's so strong. Can get on without anyone. But I was her first.

In Bangkok though there were the great gold hats of the workmen – huge, rising to a pricked point and the faces beneath red like Red Indians, slant-eyed and pointed too. Thin, thin arms. Christ, the heat as you go over tarmac! Even the girls behind the gift stalls have their heads in their arms – but they bob up and grin when they think you'll buy. The men outside are building something with a scaffolding of grass. But talk, talk, talk. The Thai girl at the foot of the gangway as we go back is tiny. Comes to my waist just about. She has eyes like small black lemons and round lips smiling. Talk, talk. Soft as a bird. Yet thin as a flake. She has a big gun in her belt.

Cassy will be drinking Nescafé. With that girl she knows who's going to Oxford. In the coffee shop in Tunbridge Wells. Or, wait a minute, it'll be tomorrow, won't it? Or will it be last night? She's that God-awful girl anyway with the brown teeth.

We are coming down low now over the China Sea. To the north is the coast of Vietnam. It is red and yellow – quite peaceful. A quiet coast. Like an orange Belgium. The sea is as still as a floor, waveless. The Mekong delta must flow into it somewhere – all that blood. All that pain. The Cambodians live in a desert now with spikes instead of trees – spikes like gibbets and holes for the twisted dead. The Cambodians were dignified people who wore top hats. Cassy and Monty used to go on about it. All those bombs and lasers and bullets. The noise of it. You'd never think, looking at that pale bit of coast –

Cassy will be –

The sky's changing. There's a great grey cumulus ahead like – God, like Europe. Like Newcastle. Or like Lille. Or like filthy Warwick. (Why didn't I stay another year at school and try for Cambridge. Christ, Warwick!)

The sun's gone. We're going down. I've been asleep. We're going down into the sea. Hey – the skyscrapers! Look at them. All of a sudden, Europe. Or Manhattan. Out there just standing in the sea! Cliffs again with rows of little holes down them, neat round holes in the great tall pencils. All crowded up together. Hey it's Lego – it's not buildings. And in between there's shacks, bits of leaves over sticks. We're nearly touching them. All the washing hanging out. Hey it's wonderful!

The vast American was asleep with the bottle and the carton, one in each hand, at an angle. The air-hostess who had joined at Bangkok whisked them out of his hands, buttoned up his tray as she went by on light feet. As tiny as the Thai but more precise, prouder. The bones of her head were minute, perfect, her quickness lovely. The Chinese alongside him had seen him thinking again, and again catching Mark's eye he bowed.

There was a Rolls the size of a room waiting, with gold headlamps and the driver in white with gold buttons. Mark's father reading *The Financial Times*, dressed as if for Chancery Lane, stood beside it. 'Dear Mark,' he said. 'I'm not long out of court. Bless you. Where's the luggage?'

With every sign of pleasure the gold and white chauffeur picked up Mark's stained sack.

'All done? All finished?' his father asked. 'Searched for drugs and all that rubbish? What a world. Well done.'

In the car they swam beneath concrete bridges, swept through streets of soft green and red and gold Chinese neon signs. The streets were being swung back and forth by great waves of small dark people all hurrying, smiling, elbowing, talking. Before

41

the hotel a fountain played, green and gold and pink by turns, in front of huge glass doors and a sugar-cake Empire façade. Little boys in white with white pill-box hats hauled back the doors like clockwork dolls. Inside a huge garden grew among the tea-tables in a circle of marble (or was it jade?) and roses and lilies and ferns and orchids were banked up in it under a glass-domed roof. At the hundred tables people sipped drinks and ate French cakes. Talk, talk. Outside by the great flight of main steps a little dark-yellow cadaver of a man, with fingers like something you suck off the bone with rice, made, magically, with small pointed movements, grasshoppers out of green leaves with baby grasshoppers woven into their backs. Mark saw not far away something else – a human head resting on a low heap of brown blankets and throught, my God, it's food! It's food for sale. They're cannibals. But the head with long matted hair turned slowly towards him. It was a Mongolian face, sleepy, peaceful and filthy. In front of the man on the pavement magazines were spread out for sale, and a rat ran over them.

'There,' said his father. 'Baggage seen to. Not much of it. Have to get you some more belongings. It gets cold here. Can you change for dinner? Doesn't matter.' He was smiling at Mark – not a word about the Arab robe, the beard and hair sticky with Cretan sand nor – good God! – the aeroplane socks which he'd forgotten to take off. His father was smiling with delight at him. 'By God, it's nice to see you, old love,' he said. 'You're three feet taller.'

'We'll go to the Kowloon when you've washed. I live in the hotel at present – since your mother left – but we won't always eat here. Get you used to some chop-sticks tonight. Tomorrow I'll take you up to have a look across at China.'

A small Chinese of such immaculate appearance that Mark thought he must be one of his father's senior partners approached, and with great reverence and pleasure held out a tray with a telegram on it.

'What's this?' said his father. 'For me? No, for you. For my son.'

'This is not one son but two son,' said the telegraph boy shaking with respectful laughter and keeping his eyes politely

42

off Mark's feet. 'One son on other son's shoulder.'

'I think I've got jet-lag,' said Mark. 'I feel a bit off.' He pulled the telegram slowly out of its thick yellow envelope. 'Crete to Athens took ages. Then at Beirut, ages. Then nine hours to Bangkok, then Bangkok –'

The telegram said, 'I love you I love you Oh I love you It is for ever Cassy.'

'You'll feel odd for a day or two,' his father said. 'The difference in time. I hope it's nothing?'

'Nothing?'

'Your telegram.'

They were being take up in a blue and gold lift to a room with twelve-foot, pure silk curtains and a bathroom of black marble.

'No, nothing,' said Mark. 'Just a girl.'

'Plenty of those,' said his father.

Mark groped for Cassy. He trod the deep carpet, looked in the bathroom. A white telephone stood on the black bath. There were five fat white towels over gold rails, an acre of mirror. Cassy was not there.

'It's fantastic,' he said, opening a cupboard full of drink, another which was a television set, another which was a stereo, another which was a desk. (Cassy was not there.) 'It's wonderful!' He looked across a bay of lights that stretched to heaven.

'I could stay here,' he said, 'a *long* time.'

They smiled at one another, man to man.

For He Heard The Loud Bassoon

I was walking down Dering Street, just off Oxford Street, after visiting the Gwen John Exhibition at the Charles d'Offay when I decided to step inside St George's Hanover Square.

It was the talbots did it. Two great stone talbots on either side of the west door – big medieval dogs with eager faces and inside-out lips. Queer things to keep outside a church. More like a country house. Very like home really. Chilbury.

Now it happens that in all my years (I'm fifty) I've not been inside St George's Hanover Square though it's been a great church for weddings. I don't mean that many people actually ask me to weddings, just the little knot one keeps up with. The rest are the same old screamers nobody knows, standing with their backs to you, necks out to the champagne. I've said to Mother – I'm asked for Mother – that there may perhaps be a special body of people one gets in for weddings – like hired mourners at Indian funerals. Mother says not. Perhaps gate-crashers, Mother says. '*Uninvited*' she says turning outward her talbot lips, sniffing with distaste the proletarian air as she indicates the march of time towards this pretty pass.

I'm asked for Mother – or who would get her home? Who'd lift her feet? 'Toby'll see to her.' I have a way of lifting her great dying legs into the car like nobody else. She can walk on the sticks but the great legs have to be lifted once I've got her sat down. Once I've got the car door shut the view of her from the shoulders up is the view of an empress.

Well.

I went into St George's Hanover Square all by myself on a Monday morning very depressed. I hadn't realised the Gwen Johns had been for sale. The show had been on three days. They'd all gone. And they had not been over-priced. And they

44

were wonderful – thin, cunning, intelligent, sexless, unfemale girls, wisps escaping, shoulders sloping, thoughtful, intricate, non-voluptuous. There were the round heads and hats of children, cats asleep deep in pillows, an old woman in a cap asleep deep in pillows, a nun like a Bellini, a glove drawn over a hand, a vellum book, skins, cheeks and foreheads luminous as Van Eyck. And all with the little red blob that means they're sold or the little blue blob that means on loan only.

I miss things.

I've always missed things. In my personal moments of decision I have always been otherwise employed. I saw it in *The Times* – this exhibition – last Wednesday. Noted it. I was hanging about with mother in the country. Chilbury. Trying to fix up her winter at Reid's, Madeira. She doesn't even *go* till January. No hurry. They know her. Keep a suite.

So I walked petulant into St George's Hanover Square and here's this very big verger with a finger to his mouth. He's in a purple cassock. Sponged and pressed. Fine figure of a man. Looked somehow well-rested.

Behind him the church was in darkness except for the side-chapel and there didn't seem to be a soul about. Quite quiet. I nodded pleasantly at the verger and he just stared back and frowned deeper and kept the big finger in place and I had a sudden very clear notion that there must be a funeral on the way.

You don't often see a funeral these days in a central London church what with all being office blocks and pied-à-terres. I mean who's going to die in Hanover Square? Or get born there for that matter? Birth and death, keep out. You can almost see it written up. 'Any sign of dawn or sunset in this square will be prosecuted.' 'Any sign of manifestation will IMMEDIATELY be towed away by the police.' But I looked round for the dreadful trestles of the funeral waiting before the altar and there was nothing. No snuffles into kerchiefs, no shuffling of heavy feet. No mourners. No flowers. The verger glared.

I have a feeble, rather rodent-like face and I grin as a rat does when nonplussed. I began to walk away from the verger, carrying my coke hat at a slight angle before me. I suppose I am the last man left in London properly hatted. I looked here and there to see what there was to see. I strolled toward the lighted side-chapel and the verger prowled behind. And I saw three people standing there in a cluster in the yellow light.

One was a priest in vestments and a very grave face. One was a tall, thin, youngish, chinless man in a silvery suit, and the third was a woman in a heavy, creamy crepe dress; no hat, but thick dark hair in short deep waves. As I came near she turned and looked at me and her mouth was very plump and sweet, her eyes beautiful and bright and excited. But grave.

She was not rich. The dress was a rich woman's dress but she had not the lines of a rich woman. Except for the dress and a sort of tension in her she might have been a Renoir.

The man turned too and he was a homosexual.

Well, it takes one to spot one as our chosen brethren tell us, and he spotted me, too. He turned back to the vicar-fellow and the vicar-fellow looked up and over at me and it then dawned on me – the first dawn for a long time in Hanover Square – that the three of them were in matrimonial attitudes.

The vicar said a quick word, bustled and billowed between the pair of them, air beneath the lace, flurried down the aisle towards me and the verger bore down beyond.

A marriage. No witnesses. Foolish young people. Banns – special licence or whatever – all in order, but no second witness. Ridiculous. People always doing it. Would I be so very kind?

So I put down the coke hat on the front pew and stood there before the altar with the pair of them. Best man. The verger looked steadily down at his feet, the hat played the mother of the bride, very quiet and controlled in the right place, and we all listened to the rounded ancient phrases.

Came the Promises. He had a good loud solemn voice, the vicar. 'Now kneel,' he cried once, and down they both flopped on two red hassocks as if they'd been shot. He took hold of a hand of each of them and held them up in the air inside one of his own, high up for me and the verger and God and the hat to see. 'LET THOSE WHOM GOD HATH JOINED TOGETHER LET NO MAN PUT –'

Well, I signed the book and the verger signed the book and the couple kissed each other very delicately and the verger vanished and the bride thanked the vicar with a big moist look and kept her hand a long time in his: and the chap – the groom – kept clearing his throat and touching the rose in his button-hole. You couldn't really get a look at his face it was so high up above everyone else's, mine in particular. I felt him looking down at me and considering the thinness of the hair across my scalp. I felt his expression of dislike. What people don't understand about homosexuals is that if it takes one to spot one warmth is not necessarily thereby engendered. Quite usually the reverse.

'This has been most awfully good of you,' he said on the steps, regarding the talbots, hardly moving his little mouth, looking away.

'*Sweet*!' she said.

'A very great pleasure,' I said.

'But such *luck*,' she said. 'Otherwise that old verger would have had to go running in the *streets* for a *traffic*-warden or something. We *are* such fools!'

The man gave something meant to be a laugh, high up among the pigeons in the portico. His head began to turn left and right looking for a cab. One came up. he signalled it. The driver, seeing the girl's lovely dress and her lighted face glowing like the Gwen John woman drawing on the glove, got out and opened the door for her.

'Do you know,' she said, turning back to me after she'd begun to get in, laughing into my rat's face under the poor streaks of hair – she was little so I suppose she couldn't see the extent of the territory – 'd'you know. I very much want to kiss you,' and she kissed me putting both arms round my neck and her round mouth very warm and soft on my cheek, not in the air to the side like most girls do if they do at all.

And I was not revolted.

'"The wedding guest stood still"',' said the groom. And she simply roared with laughter and I laughed back and the cab-driver had a bit of a smirk on too and said something Cockney in an old-world way and it was a moment of very great delight.

I didn't look at the bridegroom, however. I just turned in his direction and said, 'My very heartiest con –'

'Come with us,' he said.

'I –? What ?'

He put a pale indefinite sort of hand on my arm. '"He holds

47

him with his skinny hand",' he quoted again, surveying the bird-droppings crusted round the flagstones and the watchful dogs, 'Come with us. To the breakfast. Hyde Park Hotel.'

'Oh, of course not. Not possibly.'

'Yes. Come,' he said. 'Poor sort of wedding breakfast. No guests. Come too.'

'Do,' she said. 'Do, do, do,' so emphatically and happily, laughing again, that I said, 'But surely you -. I mean of course I should be delighted but -'

'Come,' they both said.

And there I sat. In the taxi. Mind, I sat on the flap, I made sure of that, not in between them. There we sat, I and the new-made man and wife whom no man was to put asunder. Round St James's Square we whirled, down Pall Mall, up St James, along Piccadilly, Knightsbridge and with a great flourishing and improper U-turns by the Cockney Card who seemed very taken with the whole situation, emerged before the massive silence of the Hyde Park Hotel and its discreetly glittering doors.

And he'd done things well. The groom had done things well. All properly prepared and very private. The table was ready, in an alcove, and had small special flowers. He had ordered the menu in advance and the champagne was excellent and properly cold. A third place was laid without his appearing to speak, and without a movement of a waiter's eyelid, and we all sat down and became very talkative, intelligent and interesting. We were in our alcove; an élite.

Or the girl and I were at any rate. We exuded character - quality, formality, excellence. The very expensive, rather demodée dress hung in a sort of thick droop, golden cream above the linen table cloth and the silver and the creamy flowers. For such a young woman - I suppose she was twenty-four or twenty-six - she had heavy breasts. Her shape was not fashionable at all. Her hair was deeply waved in a style which was once I believe called Marcel - there is a picture of Mother as a girl with a style like that wearing long beads and earrings. This woman wore no jewellery at all. I found that once or twice - quite often - I was looking at the heavy, beautiful dress and the shape and solid softness of her under it, and as I squeezed the lemon over the caviar I had an entirely new and entirely distressing sensation. Shatteringly it came and went as I reached for my dinner napkin. It left me shaken. I am – I don't think there has been the least question of it ever – a homosexual. Yet I longed then and there to lay my head upon the girl and sleep.

I upset the finger bowl all over the table, knocked a fork to the floor and at once got up.

The tall bridegroom watched me, still touching the rose in his buttonhole.

'What's this?' he said. He was laughing at me. I felt that his amusement comforted and eased him somehow. 'What's this?' Brows raised. 'What now?' His eyes, his mind lay open wide. He drew attention to them. 'The bridegroom's doors are open wide and I am next of kin'. 'Not going,' he said, 'after all?'

'I must –. I must –. I've just remembered. Must be mad. Meeting someone –'

She stretched a hand and said, 'Oh forget them. Forget them,' and I sat down and we drank more champagne and the waiters changed the plates.

She began to talk. She was from Perthshire. He was Swiss (the small mouth. The perfect English). Oh, the wedding was going to be such a *surprise*. Mummy and Daddy were going to be absolutely *shattered*.

I mentioned a few people in Perthshire – Mother knows a good many, but she had not heard of them. We know no Swiss, so I was unable to ask him if he knew anybody, too. It seemed rather uncivil but I don't think he noticed. He had withdrawn a little and was thoughtfully peeling grapes.

'Rolf is a banker,' she said and we all three watched the baring of the pale green flesh, the little rags of skin flicked from his finger tips onto the Royal Worcester.

'And you?' I asked.

'Oh –. I worked –. I've been in a gallery.'

'Where?'

'Bond Street. I really wanted Christies.'

'Ah,' I said. 'You'd need some qualifications for that.'

'I have qualifications.' The comforting dress and her beneath it rested against the rim of her plate of wild strawberries and her round and rosy arm.

'That on its own is not –' I had begun to blush. 'Excuse me a moment,' said the groom.

' – not enough,' I said.

'But it was before I went to Berenson.'

'To *Berenson*!'

'Yes.'

'What – in Italy?'

'Yes. That was some time ago. I was there for some years.'

Coffee came with three cups. She poured two, then looking for the husband and finding him gone put the coffee pot down at a little distance and pushed his empty cup towards it.

'I went to the d'Offay this morning,' I said. 'To see the Gwen Johns.'

She put sugar in to her coffee with precision and said without the earlier Kensington voice, 'It is an excellent collection. But I am afraid you were too late to buy. They were all sold on the first day.'

'Yes.'

'What was the price range? Do you know?' She was brisk.

'300 to 600.'

'That was not over-priced,' she said.

'I know.'

I could have wept. I wanted more than I wanted paradise or Mother off to Reid's – I wanted to rush from the room, run down the road, thunder through the Burlington Arcade, right turn and left turn and into the gallery, seize the girl with the glove, push the asses in the face at the head of the stairs, all beards and leather, talking about Promise, and run, run, run, run, all the way back and lay the picture at her feet. My eyes were wet. I bent above the coffee cup.

'Where did Rolf go?' she asked, stirring the sugar with the little silver spoon.

I said, 'Oh God, I wanted one of those pictures.'

She said, 'There are one or two more you know. I know Poppie Jones. Do you know Poppie Jones?'

'No.'

'She's about. At the gallery. She says it took ages to get just those few pictures together, but one or two more have come in. They're unhung. They're in the office at the back. Water-colours. I haven't seen them. I say – where is Rolf?'

We looked about. Waiters stood like wood.

'I'll find him,' I said. 'Are you going abroad?'

'Yes. To France.'

'I'll get him.'

I went to the gents but Rolf was not there. I had a word with the head-waiter. 'The gentleman – table nine?'

'I'm afraid I can't say, sir.'

'He'll be back in a minute,' I told her. We sat together. Her hair was almost blue in the deep parts of the broad black waves. Her eyes were dark blue too.

'Could you look again?' she said. She glanced at the clock then down at the very small watch surrounded with diamonds like a little diamond flower. 'It's getting late.'

'What a beautiful watch.'

'He gave it me. And the dress. I'm poor.' The voice at the church – the 'Do, do!', the 'Mummy and Daddy will be *shattered*', had all gone.

I went back to the gents and looked in all the compartments. I came out and put my head round all the doors in sight. I went through the glass doors and looked down Knightsbridge. I looked back across at table nine where she sat thoughtfully, the forefinger of her right hand making a map of nothing among the unused spoons. I went slowly over and stood beside her.

'Vanished for the moment. Somewhere or other. Fetching a car perhaps.'

She said nothing.

'Probably paying the bill.'

She said nothing.

'Have some more coffee. I'm sure there is heaps of time. I must be off the minute he comes back, though.'

'He's gone,' she said.

'My dear. Whatever are you talking about?'

'He's gone.' She leaned back and gave a great sad sigh and again, under the heavy dress I seemed to see her skin and feel the beating of her heart. Her eyes were not quite closed and she watched me.

'He's gay you know. Well, of course you would know. I appeal rather to gay men.'

51

'My dear girl – he's charming.'

'No. No. I mean he's a homosexual. Didn't you see? Of course you saw. I rather like gays.'

I thought that I should die. 'What rubbish!'

'I knew of course. I thought I could change him. And Bankers need wives – emblems, images – about them.'

'I'll speak to the waiter.' I ran blushing down my neck, the sweat pouring about on the top of my poor pate, runnels between the strands.

'Could I have a word?'

We moved round a potted plant.

'The gentleman at table nine ?'

The head-waiter looked at me very like Mother's doctor at Chilbury, 'Excuse me, sir. Are you a relation?'

'Well – I'm a friend. A family friend. Wedding guest. Yes, actually I am *the* wedding guest.'

'The gentleman has paid the bill,' said the head-waiter now looking more like a solicitor, executor and solicitor, able to tell the widow the one important fact: that the affairs have been left in order.

'But where – ?'

'He left, sir.'

'Left?'

'From – from where?'

'From our rear entrance I think, sir. The entrance into the Park.'

'His wife?'

He looked away, upwards, downwards. He saw of course. My voice is high. My hands were shaking.

'Whatever shall I do with the wife?'

'Might I suggest, sir – perhaps another coffee. And you might – ar – har – *pursue*?'

'Get a cab,' I said, 'and send more coffee.' I went quickly to table nine where she still leaned back but her eyes were now quite shut. 'A little trouble,' I said. 'A little nonsense. Just stay here a few moments.'

She said, 'You are good.'

I got to the doors where the cab was waiting and looking back saw her still unmoving, her hands loose now on the table with the gold ring and the diamond one and the little twinkling flower. I went all the way back over the carpet again with everyone looking carefully elsewhere and I stood by her. I said, 'Look. I shall be coming back. You do understand?' She didn't move.

I went to Victoria in the cab and then thought what a fool I was. There must be half a hundred trains going towards France. I told the cab driver to turn round and go back to Hanover Square to find the vicar. But neither vicar nor vicarage were to be found. I went into the church where every light now was out. There was a scuffling in a vestry and I found the verger, ceremonious with ewers and towels. He looked at me with no relish.

'That wedding –'

'What wedding?'

'This morning – witnesses. You and I –'

'What the gay?'

'Oh – yes. If you like.'

'I didn't like. What about him?'

'He's gone off. Left her. At the Hyde Park Hotel. At the lunch table.'

He poured water unhallowed from ewer to jug.

'Was there – ?' I said, 'Did the Vicar know – ?'

'Only they were flying to Bordeaux. Vicar held the passports.'

I got in the cab again and went to the British Air Terminal near Vincent Square and found the desk for the air terminal coach to Bordeaux and queued there for some time. 'Could you tell me,' I asked at last, 'did a Mr Rolf –? A Mr Rolf?' I realised I didn't have his name.

'No Mr Rolf is leaving for Boredeaux today.'

I took the cab back towards Knightsbridge – the meter read five pounds fifty – and I thought, my God.

'Stop,' I cried.

I paid and stood on the corner of King Street near Christie's taking slow, deep breaths. Out of my mind, I thought. Then I said it, there on the street, 'Out of my mind.'

I don't know her name.

I don't know who knows her. Or if *anyone* knows her.

I don't suppose Mother knows anyone who knows her.

I can forget the whole nonsense. I can go back home to Eaton Place, have a bath, ring up Mother, say I'll be coming down tonight. Leave the whole thing.

I could even go to a film or something. Look someone up. I'm about the last person in England with nothing special to do – able to amuse myself. The last person in England with a decent hat. I'm queer. I'm gay. Everyone knows I'm gay. I don't feel these things about women.

I banged into old Fluffy Finn-Innis on the corner of Jermyn Street. He smelled very expensive. 'My *dear*,' he said, 'have you *seen* the Gwen Johns! All gone – and gruesome, gruesome!'

'I've seen them.'

'Refined to *nothing* my dear. And each one sold. Bloodless. The place of course is packed!'

I walked back across Piccadilly and up Bond Street and in the end got to Dering Street and went into the gallery and in the office at the back I asked for Poppie Jones and to see the water-colours. Nobody knew Poppie Jones but the water-colours were there, two of them. They were beautiful and five hundred pounds each and I bought the pair.

'Are they to be hung?'

'No.'

'Then wrap them up would you. I'll take them.'

They know me there and they did and I took them under my arm in a parcel and got another cab to the Hyde Park Hotel. I rehearsed what to say. I rehearsed six versions. The first was the best.

I would get out at the main doors. I would go back through them and she would still be there leaning back. I would sit down and take her hand and pull the dainty dimity silly rings and watches off and put them in a water jug, or a potted plant –.

Or, no – I would go and sit quietly beside her and wait.

'I have brought you a present.'

'A *wedding* present?' Her sad eyes look at mine. She opens the parcel, 'Oh my heaven! Oh my heaven!'

'I hope so.'

'Whyever? I don't know you. What a queer man you are.'

'No. I'm not. I'm not a queer man. I love you.'

54

'My dear – oh my dear!' (Looking at the water-colours.)

'I want to rest my head upon you. I find I am not a queer man.'

'They are very fine – very rare. French. Touraine? Breton? Oh – even better than the portraits!'

'We might go to Rome – to Tuscany. Moscow – The Hermitage. Look – I am rich. I am not quite a fool. I am good with money. My mother is old and –. We could go to New York. At Chilbury there is still a Stubbs and –'

So I went into the hotel and the man held wide the door and the table was empty.

'The lady at table nine?'

The waiter was blank but would enquire.

'She went away.'

'When?'

'Three quarters of an hour ago.'

'Alone?'

'I can't say.'

He is looking at me. He is laughing at me. I am clutching the parcel.

'May I speak to the head-waiter?'

He approaches, noiseless, kind.

'*Yes*, sir?' We move behind the plotted plant.

'The lady at table nine? The lady who had just married?'

'Your name, sir?'

'Oh – I was the guest. The wedding guest.'

'Her name, sir?'

'I did not know her name.'

He looked very stern. 'You remember,' I said. 'You told me. We spoke. You suggested that I should ar – har – pursue?'

'I'm so sorry, sir.'

'I know it sounds a queer story.'

'Yes, sir.'

'But in fact it's not. It's not.'

'No, sir.'

'There was no message?'

'No, sir.' He looks at my pink hands on the parcel, down at the pink pig's cranium. 'I'm afraid I can't help you, sir. The

55

couple left. The bridegroom had been out for a moment from our rear entrance onto the Park. A little faint. Not quite the thing.'

And I am in the street and she is gone. The traffic rushes past making unlikely swoops and swerves. I walk up Knightsbridge – there seems to be quite a slope. I have not noticed before that it is a pull up Knightsbridge. I must go to the Agency about Mother's tickets for Reid's, Madeira. She likes things done in good time.

She is imperial from the shoulders upward, seated in her car. It is curious to see great medieval dogs outside a church.

I settle my coke hat (I am well hatted) and I walk with my unmistakable, my blatant walk, a slight movement about the hips. I'll go to the flat. Telephone somebody – maybe old Finn-Innis.

Take a bath.

But I have the pictures. I have the pictures at least.

Lychees For Tone

'Eh, Mum,' he says standing up and scratching hisself (I'm sorry but that's Tone), 'I'se bringin' a bird home Saturday.'

'Saturday's tomorrow,' I says.

'That's it,' he says bending down and pulling out the telly plug. We'd been watching the James Bond. Tell you the truth my heart were like a pump. He's twenty-two and he's never brought no girls home in his life. Tadpoles yes, lads yes. Bikes yes. And now the cars. He's dug this great hole in the front garden for the cars and lines it out with concrete. 'It's a pit,' he says. You'd think he were seven.

'Whatever you want a pit for?'

'To get at 'em,' he says. Then they drives one car or another over the pit and they crawls down underneath and they fiddles about, breaking things off and welding things on and hammering and grunting. Every night after work and half of Sundays. Transistors blaring. Saturdays is the Scramble with the bikes. Always bikes and cars and lads. Girls never.

Might be war-games to look at them on a night. In the pit. He used to play war-games when he were seven. *And* ten. *And* fourteen if you want to know. His poor father he used to go mad – machine guns racketing, bombs squealing down. 'Git out o' them bushes. If yer don't shut up I'll brae yer.' Poor Syd. He were too heavy. He should never of let hisself get upset, a heavy man like him. He just dropped down. Outside the bathroom door. Yelling at our Tony he was then, too. 'In the bloody bathroom half the morning,' he yells, and then thump and a crash and I flew. I said, 'you've done it now. You've done it this time all right,' and Tone unlocks the door and stands there all foam on his face and his shaving brush in his hand and he looks and he says, 'We'd best not shift him. Get a doctor.'

57

That's all he said and he'd killed his father.

Oh, I've been daft. I've been daft to put up with him. Not that he's not helped. He's earned good money, not like Mrs Morgan's lot. Still students at thirty hers are, writing books and that and their mother on tranquillisers.

No, our Tone pays the gas and electricity, his father not having thought ahead. No reason why he shouldn't, mind, the amount of electricity he gets through. He's got yards of these cables with electric light bulbs stuck on the ends of them, all trailed out over the garden to light up his pit. Sets them up like a blessed telly studio. Then he gets revving up the engines till all hours.

I can't face the neighbours. I mean it. I can't face them. They're foreigners both sides and they don't seem to care and they make enough of a racket theirselves but still I'm ashamed. I says to one side one day – Mrs Palmer, she's Jamaican: Mrs Morgan on the other side, on the tranquillisers, she's Welsh – 'Mrs Palmer,' I says, 'I'm that sorry about the noise.'

'I don't hear no noise,' she says.

'I mean the engines. It's my Tone.'

'Oh, we like a bit of noise,' she says. 'You ought to come and make a bit of noise yourselves when we all have a Get-Together.' Then she starts asking me to these sing-songs they have Saturday nights. She belongs to some funny Church where they all believe in love and that. So I had to draw back.

She says – Mrs Palmer – when there's more bits of cars and bikes than usual over the lawn and me just standing helpless thinking of Syd and his lobelias and the hours he used to spend on his edgings and how he wouldn't even let Tone have a rabbit-hutch out there because it left a yellow mark – 'Mrs James dear,' she says (dear!), 'that beautiful young boy of yours, he ought to have a girl-friend.'

Well, I just went into the house. I wasn't having that.

'Bringing home a bird Saturday,' he says.

'Saturday's tomorrow,' I says.

'That's right,' he says.

'And so it's me got to make the house right,' I says, 'and get food in and that?' My heart were thudding away still. I felt right queer. Excited like. Daft. I don't know why I do it somehow, the way I go on at Tone.

'You don't want your supper then?' (Saturday's his steak and kidney and a sponge.)

'No,' he says, 'I'll be getting it out. When I pick her up.'

'What, after the Scramble?'

'That's it.'

Didn't seem hardly worth bringing her home that time, I thought. And then a real terrible thing strikes me. He looks at me – great big lump. He'll have to watch his weight or he'll go down like his father – *and* sooner –

'You don't need to get owt right,' he says. 'She's comin' in with me.'

Then he thunders off to bed singing like an opera (and he has got a lovely voice, I'll say that. He could of got to the D'Oyley Carte), bumping and crashing about. When he passes me on the landing he gives me a bold great look like to say 'and there's not a blind thing you can do about it, is there?'

And there's not. All next day in the shoe shop I'm all over the place. 'Whatever's the matter with you then, Mrs James?' (Mr Hinton, the manager.) 'You're looking tired.' He's a bit sweet on me the manager if you want to know. Says I make him laugh. He thinks I'm funny the way I'm always worried. And he was good to me over Syd. He seemed to understand I was upset about not being upset, if you see what I mean. 'Enjoy yourself then, Mrs James,' he says when it's a real bad day like Sales times. 'Relax and enjoy it, Confucius he say,' and all these little girls – that Sandra! – with their great bottoms and their tight skirts lounging about while I take the customers, they just snigger. He'll be talking about tranquillisers next and have me blinkin' my eyes and yawning like that Mrs Morgan. That Sandra blinks her eyes and yawns anyway. Put her on tranquillisers and she'd drop off in a coma. She fetches me a cup of tea though, and Saturday's busy. Don't know how she stays awake to watch the kettle.

Saturday's busy. Saturday's always busy. This Saturday's murder. Thirty-seven customers and all with feet like elephants or feet like them Australian things with beaks. I used to make Tone laugh about the customers long since. Tone can laugh. Syd could never laugh. I don't believe he ever laughed at anything except in a very bitter sort of a way. 'Why do you do it then?' he used to say when I was going on about the shoe

59

shop. 'I earn good money,' he said. It's funny how he always thought he earned good money. He did maybe. He made mirrors. Unusual job. But there was none at the last. Maybe I should of packed in the shoe shop and he'd of done better. Maybe I should of been home a bit more and kept Syd and Tone apart. They did fight.

But the money come in useful for Tone's training. He were a Late Developer but good with his hands and with his figures. I don't think he'd of ever bothered to get hisself on at all if I hadn't worked to pay for his training at the engineering. He's got a lot to thank me for. His father used to say that. 'You've got a lot to thank your mother for. It's more'n I'd of done for you,' he said. 'Not reading till you was nine.'

Funny thing is Tone never looked the happier for it when I give him his money on a Friday night. Maybe I should just of left him alone.

And now this.

And he's going to sleep with her.

Just some girl or other he's picked up.

In this house. In Eastern View. His father's house. I dare say it's more like his house now since he pays the rates and that and the bit of mortgage and all the instalments. But I can't take it. I can't take it. The place his father and I went mad for, coming from Bootle, and kept decent – beautiful – nineteen years. Stepping into bed with her, just like it was on a bus!

If he's turning to this style why can't he take her to some hotel? Or go round her place? Wherever that is. Port Sunlight likely. I don't like it. I'm not used. I hear enough of it at the shop.

I wonder if he's done it before? Outside? It's possible. Things being what they are. I think I'll die. And we had him at the United Reform Sunday Schools till he were past fourteen.

I ran round home dinner time to see to his meal – best end, dumplings, potatoes, rice-pudding and treacle – and he were all togged up in his leather jacket with the studs, fixing on his round black helmet and trying to buckle on his belt. Far too fat he is.

'Did you get your dinner?'

'I did.'

60

'Was it all right for you then?'

'Grand.'

'So yer off? Scrambling?'

'I am.'

'And you'll be late back?'

'After me tea.'

I rinsed off his plates at the sink and made a cup of tea for meself and didn't look at him. He was racketing about for something.

'And you're bringing back this –?'

'I am. Where's me gauntlets?'

'How do I know where you put your gauntlets? Where she from?'

'Who?'

'This bird.'

'Oh – I dunno. Asia somewhere. She's Asian. Chinese.'

And he come over and bless me he gives me a kiss.

Well, this time I nearly did die. No wonder he gives me a kiss. Chinese! I nearly did die. I *looked* dead. I could tell by the way they all skimmered at me sideways round the shop. 'Talking to herself now,' I heard one of them say – that Sandra – in the boxes. 'Goin' on something terrible.' 'Just her age dear,' (Mr Hinton, the manager.) 'Heart of gold,' he says. That's all he knows.

Well, I gets home and it's nearly dark. They won't be that long. But there's Mrs Palmer still hanging out over my fence with the baby. One of the babies.

'Now, hello there, Mrs James,' she sings out as I puts my key in the door. 'You not happy today now, Mrs James? You ought to come to our Get-Together tonight.' She leans her whole side against the fence. Syd would of gone spare. I looks away – over at the curtains in Mrs Morgan's all drawn anyhow and not washed this side of Christmas. Thank God Syd's not here to see what's happened in this road. The baby starts laughing and clapping its hands. It's a bonny child, mind. It's a real beauty. You can't help wanting to pick it up and love it. You want to pat all that frizz. It's like the heather up above Bolton.

I says all of a sudden, 'Our Tone's bringing a girl back tonight.'

'Well now, that's nice now, Mrs James. Where she from?'

'Your parts somewhere. Asia somewhere.'

'What – is she Jamaican girl?'

'Some of them parts,' I says. 'Asia, China somewhere.'

She laughs like nobody's business. Don't know how it is, she never stops laughing. She's better off than Mrs Morgan anyway.

'Your Tone's a big boy now, Mrs James,' she says. 'Time he had a nice girl. Chinese girls make wonderful wives,' she says. 'Why not you all come round here to our sing-song?'

Well, I went in and I couldn't eat my tea. I cleaned out the kitchen. 'Let her see how to keep a place clean,' thinks I. 'Just let her see the polish on this kitchen floor. Chinese, he says. Always on about how clean they are, the Chinese. Well, let her see what clean is. You'll get nothing cleaner than Eastern View in any of your Asias.'

I'd put my top polish on my vinyl and rubbed down all my working surfaces. I went over all my blind slats – variegated pastels – and shone up my brass ornaments and washed over the leaves on the pot plant on the ledge and I looked round very satisfied. *Very* satisfied. She'll get a right shock when she sees this, thinks I. After seeing our Tone all over mud and grease she'll not think he comes from this style. She'll walk in here all little and grinny on them wobbly little feet they all have – it's their grandmothers having them in bandages. Inherited bad ankles. I read it in the *Shoe News* – and she'll look round and she'll think, My word! Here's somebody knows what's what.

I moved the plant so's her eye'd catch it first go off. Very keen on flowers the Chinese. It's like their religion, the way they arrange them about. It was on the telly. Little white hands they've got, all dainty. Never think they did a thing. Mind, all that cooking – all them little different bits – that must take a time. If they do it all themselves that is and not just open tins like they do down the Chinese take-away. I got one of them once – a tin of that stuff they eat – queer white fruits. I took it in the supermarket by mistake for mandarins. Never got round to changing it neither, come to think.

And before I knew it I went over to my store-cupboard and I got this tin out. Then I got the opener and I was opening it up. Nasty little round white things they were inside. 'Lychees' it said. Sort of slimy moth balls. Not my style. I poured them in my cut-glass fruit dish and set them down in the middle of the kitchen table.

Daft.

Then I went quick into the front room. I'm tired out from the cleaning and that and it's nearly dark now. No sign of Tone. I've got this bit of polyester and cotton I'm supposed to be making up for that Sandra in the shop, since she's got no idea. Girls can't do nothing these days. She wants a blouse and she's give me the pattern. Far too low cut.

One thing about Chinese girls is they dress decent. They don't go in for low cut like Mrs Palmer. And Mrs Morgan come to that. Nice straight backs, too. Little high collars and long sleeves. There was one in the shop today with five little ones with her all good as gold sitting on the row of chairs. Three on them still had their legs stuck out straight in front. I like to see children that size. Before their legs hang down. Up to nearly three they're like that. All colours the same.

Good as gold they were, all on them. Little pale faces and black eyes. Wonder why they're called yellow skinned? There's nothing yellow about them. Black, black eyes, shape of petals. Ten petals. Twelve if you count hers. The mother's. Didn't look much older than them, the mother. They stay young the Chinese. Still like children when they're forty. Lovely little things really.

She bought a nice pair of shoes that woman. Careful about them. Knew what she were after. Tiny little feet. And all them little things in their helmets and mittens and good coats, quiet like dolls. They'll feel the cold likely, China being the tropics. They were that *good*.

I sat there with my scissors, daft as a brush, and down the garden path I could just see in the half-dark this little trail coming. Down through our garden. To Eastern View. The five on them and this little pretty woman coming behind with two big shopping bags dragging the grass. I sees myself running out. 'Here,' says I. 'Give us hold. Mind the pit. Come here then. You can't carry that lot – all that rice and the sweet-and-sour and these Chinese Leaves you see in the supermarkets and nobody buys but stands there saying they look just as good as

63

lettuces. "Better," they say. I've said it myself, though I've never bought none. Maybe I ought. They're probably all right. Well, passable.'

I think of the fruit bowl full of them lychee things and they don't seem much to offer somehow. After a long day. I dare say that great lad's taken her out like he said he would but it'll only be fish and chips or the pub, knowing him.

Down go my scissors and I'm back in the kitchen and putting out tea and biscuits and plates and cups and the blue-handled knives that were wedding presents from Syd's sister – they were good ones. Binns's of Newcastle. The biscuit tin's got pagodas on it, black and gold. It's a thing I'd never do in the ordinary way but I leave them in the tin. On account of the pagodas. To look more friendly.

I've no china tea – she'll have to make do with the P.G. tips in the bags. Somewhere there was a willow-pattern sugar basin once but I think that cat he had broke it. He's that mad about animals I didn't dare say a word. Looking for it – the basin – I come upon these Chinese fig things in my Christmas drawer. They've been there a few years. They're a bit black. Like old bits of Syd's shag tobacco. Or used-up brillopads. Still, maybe the children'll like them.

And I sits down very sudden and I thinks, well, there it is then! That's it. They're right. You have gone off it. *What* children? The ones in the shoe shop? It's just the *one* coming – one girl. A girl-friend. His girl-friend. I'm going round the twist. Maybe I ought to go and talk to Mr Hinton –

They'll come in soon. Just the pair on them. Tone and his girl-friend. I make myself see them, step by step so's I'll be ready. Tone, the great lump – and this little girl.

Suppose she's not little, though?

She may be one of them great big fat ones. The Chairman Mao style in the siren suits. You see them on the telly all marching about in thousands with all the same haircuts, shouting out slogans and firing off rifles. Nasty angry faces they've got, too; saying how well off they are with plenty to eat and never had it so good and that. Funny really, when everything's going so much better for them why they always look so furious. They say there's nobody poor in China now. Nobody

64

hungry. No nappies to wash since there's machines and old folk to look after the children. The nappies'll be paper ones likely. There's a lot of paper in China – like rice paper. Even the houses are paper because of the earthquakes. Though that might be Japan. All the women except for the baby-minders are out growing rice or making munitions like we did in the War.

We were never furious in the War though – it wasn't slogans and firing rifles off. It was cups of tea and laughs and Workers Playtime: 'You are my Sunshine'. That style. Tell you the truth I liked the War. Syd looked grand in khaki. I met him at a Naafi dance and he looked that sensible – and crinkly hair and thin. Something after Leslie Howard if you remember. Fantastic to think he ever could of, really. He'd got all purple towards the end and he'd lost his neck. Well, it was maybe my fault. I think I irritated him.

If this girl's the Chairman Mao style we'll not get on. She'll start trying to run everything. They're the sort. You can tell. She'll be making me eat lunch and shouting slogans. Little Red Books and that. Making me get my veins done. Just to think of it makes me het up.

I pick up the lychees and I starts walking about with them thinking, 'She's not to have them. I'll put them in the fridge.'

But where's the use? Tone'll never eat them. He wouldn't touch them. Maybe Mrs Palmer might. She'd eat them. I wouldn't give them to Mrs Morgan, she gets enough out of tins already, being too tranquillised to cook for herself: but Mrs Palmer, she'd eat them. I can't bring myself just to put them down the sink somehow – first because it seems a shame when they've managed to grow them and send them all this way over the Atlantic and that, after being so poor; and second because I couldn't ever be able to press them down the sink grid. Like pressing eyeballs.

I'll give them to Mrs Palmer then. I won't go to the Get-Together but I'll just go round and knock on the door and hand them in. In a pudding basin. Not the glass dish. It was my auntie's from Southport and very good taste. It wouldn't last in Mrs Palmer's ten minutes even if they do all look like angels from heaven with heather on their heads. I'll just slip round later when Tone and this Chairman mao begins to go –. When they starts to go up to –.

If Syd was here he'd die. He'd die.

'You're not bringin' this style here,' he'd shout. When she started with her slogans he'd shout worse ones back. The Enoch Powell variety. He'd of thrown Tone out years ago anyway. Maybe I've been daft not to. Never growing up. Great daft lump. I wonder if I ought to put out clean sheets?

And I'm fiery red. Sitting here all by myself I'm fiery red.

I can't stay here. Not tonight. Well, can I? Not with them in his bed. Just across the landing. It's a small house, Eastern View. It's a single bed. It's the bed he's had since he were nine, with the oak head-board and the raised lozenge.

Well, I starts running round the kitchen putting everything away – figs and dishes and knives and pagodas. I grabs at a pudding bowl and I pounces at the lychees and I tries to decant the one into the other in mid-air so to speak and the juice runs all down my wrists and up my arm and I slip and I'm flat on my vinyl. There's broken glass and broken basin and these filthy foreign things all over everywhere, scattering and rolling for miles (It's the nylon thread runner. It never was that safe when there's been a top polish), and I lets out a wail. Spread out there on the floor I lets out a very long, awful, queer sort of a wail. My face and my dress and my tights are all over lychees. There's juice right down to my shoes and right up to my Tuesday's shampoo and set.

And I hears the front door.

Dear God, the front door!

I'm up like an ice-skater falling down in a competition and pretending he'd meant it and I'm into my coat and rinsing my hands and – let the nasty things lie there. I don't care. I'm over to the door to the back garden and I'm off. Now. Into the dark. I don't know where. I'll maybe go round and lie in the pit till morning and they'll find me dead. Tone and that great fat creature. Or the little skinny one. Loose women the pair on them. When they see me lying down that pit they'll see what morals are. They'll see I don't like it. They'll of learned something. It's not everyone thinks it's all right, they'll of learned. NOT WHEN YOU'RE NOT MARRIED.

There now. I've said it. I'm not ashamed. It's nothing to do with the sexual liberations or the race defamatory act or the women's lib. It's just it's not my style. Mrs Palmer'd laugh at me and that Sandra at the shop, she's no better, and Mrs Morgan wouldn't understand at all, being Welsh. They're very immoral, the Welsh. That's why Alfred the Great had to move them out. I heard it on Magnus Magnusson. And look at *How Green was my Valley*!

James Bond is worse, I dare say, but for him it's different, in his surroundings and with his looks. All them empty beaches and the sound of the surf and afterwards all them waiters with trays of pink gins and bits of fruit floating in them.

But Eastern View's not like that. Tone's not James Bond. You can't see James Bond's bedroom all model aeroplanes and daft Snoopy mobiles and bits of transistors. And Syd and me never. And we had chance often enough, two years courting. Round his parents every Saturday afternoon while they were at the pictures. Many a time we could of. But we never.

Bringing her home and me in the house! 'Bringing this bird home Saturday,' he says. 'Saturday's tomorrow,' I says. 'That's it,' he says.

Well then, here's my gloves and hat because I'm not nobody and I'm off. There's no one outside to see the stick on my face.

And here they come. I see his shadow first coming down the passage through the glass door with the art bubbles. I've not reached the back door.

'Where'yer off? What's that on yer face? What's the mess? What's them awful things on the floor? Looks like you been layin' eggs.'

I stands.

'Mum,' he says, 'where'yer off then?'

'Mrs Palmer's.' (Down the pit.)

'Mrs Palmer's!' He looks that disappointed. 'Aren't yer goin' to come in and see her then? She's in the front room.' His helmet's off and his curly hair's all over the place. He's got a nice face, I'll say that for him. Looks about ten when he's disappointed. Looks like he did when he brought them newts home and his father made him pour them out.

And all of a rush I sees these little black-eyed children again and they've all got curly hair. They're all round the kitchen table eating a good sponge and they're all singing – when they've put their spoons and forks together – like the D'Oyley Carte. And in nice little dresses that I've shown their mother how to run up of an evening for next to nothing. Good as gold they are, and she's out in the kitchen washing the Chinese Leaves.

I seem to have stood quiet a long time.

'I'd like to see her,' I says, a bit more dubious. 'But it's not right.'

'What's not right?'

'Me being here. I'm best away.'

'You're a good boy,' I says. 'It's you pays the instalments and it's you pays the bills. Don't think I'm not grateful. I'll just go and sleep next door with Mrs Palmer. Then I'll think what to do next.'

'Sleep with Mrs *Palmer*!' He turns purple. He has quite a look of Syd. 'Are you mad?'

'I'll go to the Get-Together.'

'You hate Get-Togethers.'

'Hold still,' he shouts, 'and I'll bring her through,' and he's off and back before I can get the door open into the garden. And he's carrying a cage.

A cage.

With a bird in it.

A bird.

'I's bringing a bird home –'

And it's the dingiest, ordinariest bird you ever saw. It's sullen-looking, bored-looking, insolent-looking, constipated-looking. It's down in the mouth. It's three parts asleep. It's probably on tranquillisers. It might be Mrs Morgan.

It's the colour of old dish-cloths – the kind you throw out. It's got a dirty blue smear down its chest like it's spilt something. It's got claws – nasty crude yellow folded leathery claws. Vicious looking. It looks at me and I look at it.

There's neither interest nor kindness nor slogans between us.

'She's Chinese,' he says. 'She's a Chinese Somethin'. Int' she a beauty?'

'You'd of said no if I'd asked you,' he says in a bit, and I sits down heavy on my leatherette foam-top. I sits heavy.

He says, 'Look, Mum. I'll see to her. Have her down here with you if you like.'

'She'll be company,' he says. 'I'll see to her. She'll mek no extra.'

I sits heavy.

'Mum,' he says, 'look, she's yours if you want her. I knows you gets lonely. Look, she don't *have* to be in with me.'

Well I cried.

The Dickies

'If it ever comes up,' I said to Dickie, 'if ever you happen to mention that you saw me, could you say I was alone?'

He replied, 'Could you say I was not?'

The first time I met the Dickies and the only time I ever saw them together was in Pam Foxley's garden this side of Guildford on a June evening when we had all been invited there to dinner.

Pam lives in a pretty house – The Rookery, though she has successfully discouraged birds – all beams and black metal window-frames and prints and pelmets and dogs. She's a widow. I don't know anything about her husband except that he died all of thirty years ago. It is generally assumed that she didn't think much of him, though as she has never done a day's paid work in her life he must have been well-heeled and that usually rates pretty high with Pam.

She is my mother's friend rather than mine. She has little in common with my mother except that they are constantly on the telephone to one another about things like does she remember Mabel Crawford and if so or even if not would she be able to put her up for a few nights as she's coming to Sloane Street to have her dog done over.

Pam and I have nothing in common at all. She boils down – she has boiled down and been removed from the heat: she is a reduction, a glaze – to everything I most dislike. She hates children, blacks and Jews. She despises education and the working man ('Of course I can tile a bathroom. If *they* can tile a bathroom then I can. If they could do anything better they wouldn't have that sort of job, would they?') and I don't think she has ever read a book. When anyone breathes the faintest whisper of the arts or the sciences in her presence she cries out, 'Oh, I say! Brainy.'

Her time is arranged pleasantly and well in advance and according to the Surrey social almanac: Chelsea Flower Show, Henley, Wimbledon, Motor Show, Ideal Home Exhibition and Harrods at Christmas where because she lives just within the limit she makes their vans deliver free all her little Christmas boxes of handkerchieves separately gift-wrapped. She gets a kick out of watching the pence and cares like a new mother about her possessions, a new woman about her rights. She goes to church on Easter Day because it is the thing to do.

That she thinks it is the thing to do gives Pam away as being pretty old. I don't know how old: perhaps seventy – but she is trim, well-dressed and spare, with a good perm and plenty of hair in the right places. Driving her car full of meals-on-wheels she might well be fifty. Jane Austen said that you are pretty clear of being desired by the time you're fifty-five but she might well have thought again had she met Pam. A classy driver in her Ford Capri, I have seen men look at Pam with respect and interest as they've caught up with her momentarily at traffic lights too blatantly at red for even Pam to disregard. She's a Betjeman girl.

But the really powerful thing about Pam is her relentless friendship. Unless people are children, blacks or Jews – or brainy – she is totally uncritical and once introduced or perhaps once you have invited her to something which you quickly do because Pam is so confident and good-looking that she's very good company – there you are on her list. She will never, never drop you.

She will also begin to change you. You will begin to grow boring, slow down, stop thinking, let the scene roll by – or so it seems to me, because there must surely be someone in the whole of the rhododendron set in Surrey interested in something other than food, dogs, television and maids-before-the-War; people for whom birth and death, marriage, and fork-luncheons must hold significance and not just occur, leaving behind them neither wreckage nor delight. Pam's people must at times belly-laugh, weep, turn their face to the wall, pick their teeth or nose, place a finger in an ear and shake it about, scratch the top of

71

their legs, copulate, write unwise letters, keep drink in the wardrobe, cling, have fantasies, occasionally wonder, at funerals which they are always attending, about the hereafter or the Nature of God.

Yet you'd not know it. Pam's luncheons have bred it out of them and on her stage the characters behave as formally as the characters of Congreve, only substituting for the brilliance a steady settled dullness that is – so one hopes – as unnatural as persistent wit.

She has a lot of power, Pam. She makes you feel easy and English and secure and that though life can sometimes be a bit of a bore it is – with the help of a stiff upper lip and a gin or two – worth keeping on at. No poor people come to Pam's house.

She manipulates and modifies – at least she certainly manipulates and modifies me. I'd never wear long earrings at Pam's for instance or a dress I feel to be exciting. The day before I go to lunch with her I look out a tweed skirt. I may even press it. I have been known to turn back for a different pair of shoes. And then to turn back again to polish them. Pam's is the sort of place you have your hair done for. The fumes of the setting lotions can render her tiny diamond of a dining-room almost overpowering. I have painted my nails for Pam, attached the odd Balmoral lapel pin. I appear there appropriately, for there is something that I fear – the inappropriate being noted, considered, remembered, the feeling that I have lost marks. Pam is a perfectly dreadful woman.

She is also kind. She'll be your first visitor in hospital and if you have anyone ill at home, even a child my mother says – particularly a child now I come to think of it – she will ring up not once but twice and usually have sensible advice about it. If something happens not recognised in Rhododendria except by bright laughter or total blankness – you are breathalised and in the *Evening Standard*, you are unwise with somebody's husband, you make a scene at a Bridge: next day it will be Pam who is on the telephone while all the others are crossing you off, to say she's found just the thing to take your tea towels in your new kitchen to keep them out of sight – even though she won't have seen your kitchen for six months and you've ceased to consider it new and the tea towels now take their chance in the dog's basket. Pam has a supply of those black savage-looking salad servers – I think they're Christian Aid – from Borneo and she doles them out just as you're silently groaning that there's all the washing to do and she's asked herself to lunch. She's remembered that you've never had salad servers because you're too scatty to buy any and always make do with wooden spoons. Guest towels proliferate with Pam. She dumps them on the hall table wrapped in brown tissue paper as she leaves and they always match your bathroom walls.

She's brave, too. She dealt with a mastectomy without mentioning it until afterwards and I looked in her bathroom cupboard once and saw a whole range of bottles and pills marked 'Royal Marsden Hospital – repeatable'.

But this story is about the Dickies.

We were sitting before dinner, my mother and I, in Pam Foxley's garden each with a gin and tonic, each in a shiny white Peter Jones garden chair with identical chairs facing and a gleaming white garden table in between, and Pam for a moment indoors dealing with gravy. Round the corner of the house and under the rustic trellis with its purplish roses – all spaced out at intervals like on one of Pam's firescreens – there suddenly ran a shrieking woman.

She was elderly though still shapely and ran on elderly still shapely legs. She had rather coarse flying grey hair which she tossed from side to side. She was followed by a large fat man who was smiling.

I suppose you can still just say that an Englishman has a military appearance and be understood. Dickie had a military appearance. He was big, clean, authoritative, handsome and nice. He had a firm attentive handshake and kind quiet blue eyes. I took a great liking to him and looked forward to an evening on the Western Desert and the Sicily landings – though Pam told me later he had in fact never left his Bank.

From Pauline Dickie however I reeled back. I almost literally reeled back because I had made the mistake of standing up to be introduced – always a tricky matter in Surrey – by Pam who had come out of the house at precisely the right moment carrying nuts. My mother had wisely remained seated but even so seemed affected by the onslaught of Mrs Dickie, seemed pressed back into her chair as by a blast.

'My dress!' cried Mrs Dickie without acknowledging us. 'My dress! Oh lor, Pam, I must *disappear*!' Her voice was very queer and high and loud and her big long body wriggled about. She began to back away across the lawn giggling in a way that reminded me of something. 'Zip gone! Stuck! Help!' she called from under the roses, 'All his fault.' She pointed at Dickie who had sat down still quietly smiling. 'Must take it off!' she cried and vanished.

I thought, 'I know. It's school. She's playing schoolgirls. She's way past fifty. She's pathetic.'

'Cigarette?' asked Dickie.

He leaned towards us with a cigarette case from Dunhill's which had 'P to Jo-Jo' across the corner in curly script. Pauline Dickie's head appeared from the mat of polished creeper that surrounds Pam's bedroom window.

'Pam – I want some *nail* scissors.'

'All right,' said Pam, 'coming. Can you do the drinks, Jo-Jo?' and she went quickly into the house and returned with Pauline Dickie who was now wearing one of Pam's floaty twenties dressing-gowns and carrying her dress and the nail scissors.

'No thanks,' she said. 'No gin. Nothing till I get this *zip* unstuck. All *his* fault. Told him he'd ruin the evening. Got in the car unzipped and said "Zip me" and he gives a great heave and it sticks! At the top with a great gap showing. All my knickers, dears *and* my bra straps!' She tugged and yanked at the zip fastener and wriggled frantically under Pam's pink crêpe. The mixture of coyness and resentment, girlish movements in hands grown bony, wiry old hair like a menopause Ophelia – was awesome.

A very short silence fell and Dickie who was still smiling said, 'Pam – come along. A drink. You've been cooking,' and getting up put a hand on Pam's shoulder. Pauline at once begun a monologue about how they had thought they would be late and it was all Dickie's fault because he would not get out of his gardening clothes. My mother said that her late husband had

74

been just the same and then everyone remembered that I had not a husband to refer to as he had left me (Pam is far too experienced a hostess not to have warned the other guests), and I could feel the difficulty registering with Pam and Mother and Dickie though Pauline Dickie was hacking away with such concentration – conscious concentration – that she wouldn't have noticed if the rest of us had lain down on the grass and died.

'Do you have a garden?' Dickie asked me.

I said yes we had and I'd nearly been late myself. I had been spraying roses against black spot. I had been in the garden all day.

'I told her she'd be late for Pam's,' said my mother. 'She knows nobody dares be late for Pam's.'

'Don't know what you mean,' said Pam.

'Oh yes you do, dear,' said my mother, 'You'd have given us hell.'

'I have black spot this year,' said Dickie, looking me straight in the eyes.

I said, 'You sound like Blind Pugh.'

It wasn't the sort of joke you make at Pam's. He gave a great delighted laugh and I met a quite different look from his bland eyes – sharp and surprised as if I had felicitously muddled my lines.

'We're all going to be late,' said Pam, 'if we don't go in to dinner in precisely one minute.' She looked at Pauline, 'Come on or are you going to eat in my kimono?'

'I'd love to eat in *deshabillé*,' said Pauline pronouncing it like a measurement of the volume of sound. She stuck out a long leg from the midst of Pam's frills. It was bony and grey and a painful-looking blue vein bubbled down the calf. 'Oh golly,' she cried, 'I nearly got it then.'

'At least,' said Dickie, 'Blind Pugh didn't have leaf-curl. Have you got leaf-curl?'

'And green fly,' I said. 'And rust.'

'I don't know what you two are talking about,' said Pam, and Pauline shouted, 'Ha!'

It was a bitter sort of cry and we all looked at her but it seemed

75

she was only meaning the zip fastener which now sailed free and she ran off in to the house and reappeared for Pam's soufflé – perfection yet only four eggs – in the dress, which we all noticed was much too tight and cut harrowingly low. Above it her face looked very set and her hair more dishevelled than ever.

She became, as we went from the soufflé to the lamb, quiet. Pam was busy with the heated trolley and vegetables, Dickie with the wine. My mother talked on about nothing in particular, and I sat wondering as usual how Pam kept her silver so shiny and why there were no blemishes of any kind on her two-hundred-year-old dining table: but Pauline Dickie's silence dominated the room.

I tried to talk to her. She hardly bothered to answer. She looked out of the window, fiddled with forks and in the middle of something I was saying broke in and shouted at Pam that she hoped it wasn't going to rain because she could see that their car-windows were open.

'Jo-Jo can't shut a window to save his life!' Jo-Jo laughed easily.

It occurred to me that Pauline was waiting for something, a curtain of some kind to go up so that she could start a performance. I remember wondering if she belonged to some amateur dramatic society and if so whatever parts they gave her. It seemed to me, too, that Dickie was anxious to postpone things, was wearily trying to hold the lights, and it was almost with a sigh it seemed to me – we had reached the fresh fruit salad and Pam's soft-centred miniature meringues, exactly two each – that he leaned forward and for a second placed two fingers on my wrist and said 'Cream?'

I say a second not diminutively. A second of hand-touching on open table top at a small dinner party in Rhododendria is long. I said no thanks I didn't like cream very much and passed it on.

My mother said, 'She's never liked it. Not even as a child – nothing to do with her figure. She's just silly.'

'I can see,' said Dickie gravely, 'that it's nothing to do with her figure,' and across the table Pauline Dickie sent one of Pam's Royal Doulton cheese plates spinning to the parquet with a crash.

'Oh Pam! Oh Pam,' she cried, 'I'm so sorry. Oh I'm such a muggins.' Pam looked livid and my mother began to mop about with a napkin – some wine had gone over too, and Dickie had patiently risen and edged himself round the narrow space and bent down to try and pick up the bits.

'Oh leave it. I'll do it. It's all my fault.' Pauline pushed him so that he tottered.

We had coffee in the sitting-room quickly after that, Dickie taking some time to join us – I heard him talking to Pam in the kitchen – and as I stood looking out at the twilit and un-diseased roses and the white chairs gleaming in the dusk, I wanted very much to go away. Mother was talking to Pauline Dickie over by the fireplace and Pauline Dickie sat morosely, bony chin in hand, a grey lock across the eyes. Dickie and Pam rejoined us but before the brandy mother decided that she had left our keys in the door at home and we must get back at once. Mrs Dickie didn't get up as we left, just turned her face towards us with a tired smile, though Jo-Jo made a great point of seeing us right to the car, shook hands with very good will and hoped that we would all meet again.

I rang Pam the next day to thank her for the evening and try to hear some more about the Dickies, but she was out. I tried again and she was engaged and then I forgot about it. It was nearly a month later that she telephoned and asked me to meet her from the Wimbledon tennis and take her to Waterloo.

It seemed to me that it would be much easier for her to go back by walking to Wimbledon station and catching the train from there which was presumably the way she would have come, and especially since I live in Hampstead, but Pam seldom asks anything and I've had dozens of lifts from her, so I set out on the hottest evening of the year into the fraught landscape of Parkside and Victoria Drive on the evening of the men's finals.

I sat stuck among the motor coaches and the ice-cream sellers and messengers of doom with banners until Pam stepped all alone out of the crowd in a linen dress, two strings of pearls and a hat. She noticed my shoes which were not what she called driving shoes, then said, making the reason for my journey clear, 'Could we just look in at Putney?'

Pam never brings her car to London in case it gets scratched and in Putney as I have not yet mentioned she has a gigantic Lesbian daughter called Felicity who hasn't much time for her.

'I haven't seen her since the Tennis last year,' said Pam. 'Makes it easier if I have someone with me.'

We edged round Tibbett's Corner and painfully and slowly down Putney Hill, in a fumy trail of cars, mopping our faces with handkerchieves. I remembered that I had not thanked her for the dinner party.

'No,' she said, 'you didn't and neither did your mother.'

'I'm terribly sorry. I've never forgotten before. I was a bit fussed that night. So was mother.'

'Yes.'

The thank-you note or phone call is as integral a part of Pam's summer – or winter – formalities as the one and a half bottles of wine, the chocolate peppermint in the coffee cup saucer, the two kinds of nuts with the gin. Forgetting would not be forgotten. I felt very ashamed.

'Your mother hadn't left her key in the lock you know,' she said. 'I saw it in her bag. I didn't say anything. I thought she was probably wanting to get away.'

'Mother's getting on,' I said and remembered she is probably younger than Pam. 'Those Dickies,' I said fast. 'Were they – ?'

'You're going to meet one of them again in a minute,' she said. 'Glad you liked them. Thought you would.'

When we drew up outside Flicky Foxley's house I looked at it with new eyes. Neither Dickie seemed a likely occupant.

'Are the Dickies friends of Flicky,' I asked, wondering why Pam's friends had such names, 'Or is it Dorothy?'

'Neither. I had to send the woman somewhere. She wouldn't come to me.'

'*Send* her – ?' I said but the door opened and Dorothy, Flicky's friend, put her head round it somewhere down by the knob and said,

'Thank goodness! Are you going to take her away?'

'Where is she?' Pam went into the living room while Dorothy stood looking helpless in the hall. I never understand about Lesbian relationships. Flicky Foxley has the build of a stevedore and the feet of Michelangelo's David and Dorothy looks like a wayside posy, yet it's Flicky who wears the diamond ring. I've always felt uneasy with Flicky, but Dorothy, until I remember, I feel I could hug. She's like an old innocent teddy bear, the kind you keep on your bed until long after you should.

Well – I don't know what goes on. I gave up wondering long ago. I was at school with Flicky and I kept my distance. She was always sobbing in the cloakrooms.

Dorothy drew me beseechingly to the kitchen.

'Oh,' she said. 'This Pauline Dickie!'

'Yes,' I said, 'I've met her. And her husband.'

'You've *met* him. You've *met* him! Oh, but what a monster!'

'He didn't seem a monster. I liked him very much.'

'Oh women do, women do,' said Dorothy confusingly, clasping her small hands together, 'That's it. That's the trouble. He's dreadful. *Insatiable*' (in a whisper). 'It's one after another. Always has been. She's taken absolutely all she can.'

Felicity came marching by to get the sherry decanter and handed me an eyes-right and a curt nod in passing.

'Bad business,' she said. 'Still, I think we'll get her back. Not sure how wise it is of course.'

'Did she leave him?'

'Had to. No choice. Simply impossible. Went off with some woman after a dinner party. Pretended he was shutting her car-windows. Blatant. He'd only met her once.'

I said the only time I had met Dickie had been at a dinner party where I thought he had been very good to her. She had been behaving like a neurotic teenager, I said, and if Flicky wanted to know I hadn't been able to stand the woman.

'There are worse things than teenagers,' said Flicky. Thrusting out her jaw like Winston Churchill she said, 'Part of us all is still a teenager.'

'No part of me was ever like Pauline Dickie.'

'Oh hush – she'll hear,' said Dorothy.

In the sitting-room Pauline was curled up largely on one end of a greasy William Morris sofa (Why do male homosexuals so often live in band-boxes and female ones in rubbish bins?) holding a handkerchief across her eyes as if she were about to be shot.

'Could you give Pauline a lift to Waterloo too?' asked Pam. I said yes without enthusiasm and we all sipped sherry.

'Well, get your coat Pauline,' said Pam, 'Get it now. Don't start thinking again.'

There came a long moan, and a meaning look passed between Flicky and Dorothy. In the hall Pam was gathering up Pauline's suitcase and Flicky, feet apart, put her hands behind her back and looked out of the window. Dorothy went over and tweeted at a bird in a cage.

'Oh come on,' called Pam. Looking at nobody, eyes abrim, Pauline walked to the door, out of the house and into my car.

'Well, good to see you, Flicky.' Pam was robust. 'Anything you want doing? Any sewing?'

'Sewing?' said Flicky fiercely and Pam got into the car with an awkward crippled sort of movement and dropped her gloves. The only time I ever see Pam rattled is in Putney. Flicky went back into the house slamming the door, leaving Dorothy bobbing on the gate.

I drove as fast as one can in Tennis Fortnight down Putney High Street and the King's Road trying not to hear the dreadful snufflings in the back. The car felt hotter than ever. Pauline was wearing a dress very high-cut under the arms. Yet at Waterloo Pam helped her out carefully and seemed to be ignoring me.

I said goodbye and that I really was sorry not to have thanked her for the dinner, but she just said,

'That's all right. You might show a bit more of something or other now though.'

'What?'

'Well, speak to the poor thing.'

I looked across at Pauline, propped like a dead lily by the ticket office. I said, 'Oh Pam, she's awful.'

'That has nothing to do with it.'

'But he'll be there when she gets back. She's not alone. You're not saying much to her yourself.'

'I'm old and I'm not good at it,' said Pam.

In September I forgot the Dickies and Pam Foxley and the Putney ladies because my husband came back and we decided – in what would have been my mother's or Pam Foxley's phrase – to try and make a go of it again. The attempt was to be private and I told my mother that I had decided to take a holiday in

France alone. After saying that to be alone would do me no good and why didn't we make up a little party – for instance, Mabel Crawford – she decided it would be a good chance to have some people to stay in London herself using my bedroom and seeing some shows. She hadn't been able to go out much since I had come home. Now that I was better Mabel Crawford and her hairdresser had said it was time she had a little break. I agreed. They were quite right there.

So Giles and I caught the Newhaven Ferry and sat on deck on a hot, still morning looking at the bright haze over the sea. Giles read and I sat beside him. The boat was not crowded – the holiday season was over and the few people passing to and fro, either because of the September light or my great happiness, all looked beautiful. I turned for my bag on the deck to get a camera and found myself looking through a porthole in the state-room behind me straight into the face of Jo-Jo Dickie.

Immediately the curtains were pulled shut across it.

I said, 'Oh!'

Giles said, 'What?'

I said, 'There's someone I know in the state-room.'

'State-room? Are there still state-rooms? On a ferry?'

I said I supposed so. There must still be people who would pay extra to be private.

'Through the nose I should think,' he said. He turned and saw the closed curtains. 'Whoever is it? Was it?'

'A man I met out at dinner.'

'Is he a spy or something?'

'I shouldn't think so. He's supposed to be a sex-maniac. I met him at Pam's.'

'At *Pam's*! A sex-maniac at Pam's!' It pleased him so well that he laughed at it at intervals all the way to France, for he was finding his book insufficient and not concentrating on anything very much. I felt quite grateful to Jo-Jo Dickie I remember because he was making Giles laugh.

We didn't see anyone come out of the state-room as we left. He wasn't in any car near ours as we drove off the ship and I forgot him altogether in the familiar ramshackle reckless smell of France.

Eating our picnic – pâtè, cheese and wine: Giles is marvellous at choosing cheese – I did remember him. Two hundred miles south in a field of sunflowers I wondered who it was Dickie had had with him in his state-room: and hoped it wasn't Pauline.

Yet somehow I could not imagine what sort of woman it could otherwise be.

'Just anyone,' they had said. 'He goes off with just anyone. His wife suffers dreadfully.' And he had put his fingers publicly on my wrist at dinner which nobody had done for a long time – for nothing makes one less provocative than being deserted, whatever people say.

Sometimes people will flatter a deserted woman out of kindness, but I'm not the sort people are kind to. Mother says I am frightening because I look too composed. And I have never been able to talk about Giles. Never to anyone. It was a long time before even mother knew what had happened and then only after intensive nonchalant enquiry and a lot of tele-phoning to people late at night when she thought I was asleep.

I did tell Pam. As I've said it is difficult to keep things from Pam, especially if she is expecting them. At once I very much wished I hadn't because she gave me a hard stare and took me off to Barker's sale to buy double sheets as a distraction. Single sheets, she said, are a bad bargain. One is always wise to buy double. It was so typically insensitive I thought, that I went, and found it all bizarre enough to be glad that I had.

No – Dickie's attentions I felt quite sure had not been in the nature of an invitation. I remembered him looking straight at me when I'd mentioned Blind Pugh and the look had been comradely. I had felt that he saw that I might be thought attractive, that I was wanting to keep my distance and that I was wretched. He had liked my joke and that was all. The fingers at the dinner table were – what were they? I looked at Giles's long fingers on the steering wheel now. He took a hand off the wheel and held one of mine. Giles would touch someone's – anyone's hand at any dinner, but old Dickie –. Old Dickie doing it was as much out of character as a general deciding to sit in his braces at a regimental dinner.

The reason Dickie had held my hand, I thought, – we had reached the South now; it was after dinner and I was in the hotel garden on a lovely evening looking at an orchard full of red apples and an apricot wattle-and-thatch farmhouse and Giles had gone to make a phone call – the reason Dickie had touched my hand was because he was expected to. Pauline, I thought the next day – we were leaving early and Giles was paying at the desk for we were returning home – Pauline had wanted it.

In Paris Giles and I said goodbye and I took a plane for Heathrow and was there in not much more than an hour – Giles would still be motoring northward towards Dieppe, the ferry still ahead of him. He had caught a cold. The weather had broken. In Paris it had been already raining and cold and Giles had had no coat – his girl-friend had not thought of one. Not – since he had then been coming back to me – that she had probably been in charge of his packing. Giles's own attempts at packing had been one of our oldest jokes. Well, maybe now that he was going back to her she would look after him better.

It only occured to me as I came out of the 'Nothing to Declare' – I suppose I must have been through it because I seemed to have collected my case off the roundabout and here it was in my hand – that Mabel Crawford had my bed and I had nowhere to sleep that night. For the past six months I had kept away from friends. I could go to some hotel but could think of none. I wasn't starting my new job which had been planned to be simultaneous with my re-marriage until next week. So I had absolutely nothing to do and nowhere to go. I walked along the cold glass corridor echoing with rain, past the boulevard of glass doors and put my head in one of the chill plastic buckets there and telephoned Pam.

'I'll meet you,' she said. 'Don't worry. No, of course. I won't ring anyone. Not interested. Get on the tube. I'll be at the station. It'll take you less than two hours,' and when I got out of the train there she was in her heather-mixture suit and a felt hat. Her mouth looked rather more lined than usual, pursed up with distaste, and she was talking vigorously to a Jamaican porter who was blowing his nose but not finding her unentertaining.

The rain came down. The porter's cold was reminiscent of Giles's. His long leanness and brownness and his unwise lack of a coat had me suddenly by the throat and I began to weep.

'You see,' said Pam spotting me, 'here's a young English-woman with a cold and she's been on holiday in the South of France. If *we* are all full of cold you are bound to be. You would be much better in the country where you were born.'

'That's here,' said the Jamaican.

'Well take her case anyway,' said Pam, 'and these Beecham's Powders. And hot lemon – *hot*. Get in the car, child – there's roast chicken.'

'For dinner,' she said.

We hurtled off into the soaking landscape, rain flowing off grass verges, the sad borders of dashed michaelmas daisies – and I cried all the way to The Rookery while Pam talked loud and long – about Flicky I seem to remember, and Dorothy, who were in some new throbbing dilemma, Dorothy having shut herself in the bathroom with the bird.

'I can't understand that sort of thing,' said Pam. 'Never could. This sex business. I'll not be any help to you now if it's sex I'm afraid. Can't give advice. I never *liked* Flicky. I dare say I shouldn't say so – my only child. I can't stick children. Never know what to say to them. They all seem so – brainy. Even my own girl. Foxley was brainy of course – Jews are – and if he hadn't gone and died. That was the trouble. Since Foxley died I've been a bit of a – Well, a bit of a dry stick I suppose.'

I realised through all this that Pam was telling me something unlikely about herself and I had not stopped being astonished when she told me something more unlikely still.

'You're the only child I ever liked,' she said. 'You were a very nice child. You're a bit like me. Can't talk. Difficult. Bit abrasive. Getting hard. You ought to get right away. From your mother. Feather cushion.'

'She's been wonderful,' I said. 'Wonderfully kind.'

'Oh, *kind*,' said Pam with disgust. 'You need another man.'

At the front door of The Rookery – smoke from the chimney, lights behind the diamond panes, first leaves of autumn rattling on the wall – she said, grabbing my case, 'By the way Jo-Jo Dickie's here. Not staying long, but he waited. He has to be back because of Pauline. She's having a bad time with him just now.' Then she went upstairs to unpack my suitcase and make a note of all my new nightdresses.

Dickie passed me a drink. Genial as ever he watched my hand shake. He looked utterly relaxed, formal and calm.

He said 'Trouble?'

'Yes.'

'But you will come through it. You are very young.'

Then he said, 'He was very self-centred and I should say arrogant.'

'Did you see him?' My drink slopped over.

'Yes, I did.'

The noise of Pam and bathwater and dogs upstairs became tremendous. I said – it was the first time that I had ever discussed Giles with anyone on earth 'Giles is a man who finds it difficult for – one woman to be enough.'

Dickie said, 'I find one woman almost too much.'

We looked at each other and after a while I smiled at him because I had suddenly understood him, and he smiled back as if he knew. It was the way he had said it. He had told me his burden.

He loved Pauline. He loved her, but about being loved and about loving Pauline was not at all particular, because what Pauline wanted was not love at all, but pity. As other women want love she wanted pity. Dickie loved her and understood her and so much that he was able to play the most difficult of all parts, the unwilling philanderer; and it must have kept him in an utter and continual weariness.

I said, 'Who was it with you on the ferry?'

'Oh, no one,' he said. 'I have to go off quite a good bit you know. Not for long. But quite often. She – expects it. She's a bit of a crazy old joke you know.' He looked at his watch and said he'd have to be off in a minute. 'Half an hour late's about right.'

'Does Pam know?'

'Who's sure what Pam knows?'

I said, 'Don't you feel that one day – one day, you'll just not be able to go on?'

He said, 'Oh no.' He rocked about on his toes and looked severely into his drink. 'There are great disadvantages. For instance I would so very much like to see you again. And – you'll understand – it is not possible.'

There was more sound of Pam on the stairs, to let us know she was coming, and hearing her I felt that I understood her, too: that Pam for me and for Dickie and for goodness knows how many others represented something unchanging and strong and good. I would never talk to her about Giles but she would never need to know. She was not a deserter.

Before she got into the room I said to Dickie, 'Look – if you ever happen to mention – if it ever comes up that you saw me on the ferry, could you say I was alone?'

He said, 'Could you say I was not?'

The Great, Grand, Soap-Water Kick

Now and then you get to get washed. Now and then you start needing bath.

Not often. Every second year maybe.

Comes over you. Sudden. You begin think, hullo now. Sun hot. You see big toe lookin out of slit boot, yellowish grey. Like ivory. On elephant.

People start moving away.

I'm tramp, see. Hobo. Drop-out. Gentleman of road. Swagman. Tramp. May have seen me on road anyday fifteen years. Push pramalong. Full gear. Got long black coat. Rags other clothes under. These not see for many years at time. Not observed. Between these and skin lining newspapers. The news is old. Keep all about me, day night. Pushing pram.

Stop. Have good burrow. Rubbish bins. Sleep park, steps cinema, back church, back seat parked car. Places people gleaming faces nothing do hand soup bread. Grand what pick up too.

Name Horsa. Daft silly woman mother. Dead all I know. Hengist dead too. Julius Caesar dead. Napoleon, Churchill, Harry Pollitt, Hitler.

Dead. Horsa sixty. Maybe seventy. Give take year. Never count up.

Until start thinking wash. Comes on like said – slow, slow.

Hot day. Wash.

Water. Wash.

Wash. Bath.

Soak. Steam.

Grand.

When boy, town called Nevermind (Mugstown, Mutstown) one good thing. Bath. Oh boy! Someone scrubbing away ears,

back, toe-nails pure pink-white, shiny. Not elephant slab-grey.
SO.

Go this day down road town maybe Mugstown, Mutstown all
I know. Get there over hill, through wood, up village, out
village and it was raining. My rain! Deepest Paper under-
linings wet as sump and soggy.

Rain turn snow. Horsa shacks up barn. Farmer looks. 'Get
out there, you or I'll getmegun.'

So pushoff. Pram sticks every tenyards icy mud. Sits down
splat. 'Great goodfornowt,' yells farmer. 'Firing hay bloody
fags.' 'No fags,' says Horsa. 'Don't smoke, farmer,' but comes
out bad: 'burble-wurble-yah-blah-splot.'

Tramp, see. Loner. No practice mouth, tongue, vocal
cordage of sarcophagus.

'Bad words, filth!' yells farmer. Horsa steps on. Staggers on.

That night hedge back, bath idea begins rise. Begins simmer.
Dog comes up sniffs. Howls. Runs off.

Bit high, Horsa. On high-Horsa. Time go.

What do is this. Look for house good class, empty. Look see
water pipes growing up walls. Pass nowagain maybe week and
watch what goes.

He goes out.

Kids out.

She goes out.

Twelve clock she back.

Maybe Fridays or somedays she always later. Maybe teatime.
Maybe keepfit, yoga, coffee Mugstown friends.

So after two Friday, on Friday three in nips Horsa, first
hiding pram outhouse, garden shed, find way bathroom, start
in. Oh boy!

So finds this house, oh verynice. Verygoodclassperson. Green
grass of Mugstown well-cut, metal-edges. Keep grass not feeling
too fullofself. Keep place. Gravel paths of mustard yellow.
Windows white nets, swags like innertent. Front door smart
boxsweets. Good chain for pullbell.

He goes out.

Kids go out.

She goes out. Big bag so out all Mugstown day.

Up steps goes smelly Horsa pulls chainbell.

Now if one comes, one Gran, one serving-maid, one lodger one mad aunt kept close within, says Horsa, 'Besogood. Give poor tramp glasswater,' which sings out 'Wurble-burble-splash-woosh-splot-PAH,' and Horsa screamed upon, yelled upon, scourged upon, sentonway.

But if no answer then it's the great, grand, soap-water kick. Oh boy!

SO.

Up steps – pram hidden safe below. Nobodybout. Road dead nine-thirty clock o' the morning. Nice quiet houses, nice quiet burglar-alarm red boxes just stand. Inside each, all tables, chairs, clocks, pictures sit looking each other warm-clean out of wind, rain, weather, poor sods.

Up steps smelly Horsa.

Rings bell no answer.

Ringsgain no answer.

Ringsgain turns look updown. Not living soul. Not motor car. Not bike. Only cat gatepost watch through yellow slits. Cat stands, stretches on four fat sixpences, turns round, curls upgain, goes sleep. 'Carry on Horsa. Have bath.' Like cats. Clean, interesting.

Round back house kitchen window open. Thought silly woman. Right. Water taps inside window knobbly, window small. Horsa big. Yuge. Elephant Horsa. Horsa the elephant tramp. Horsa theyear. (Hobo. Drop-out, Gentleman road. Swagman. Scrappy. Tramp. Oh boy!)

Maybe left something else open like perhaps back door? Don't bedaft Horsa. Not your luck and you are lucky. Kick three milk bottles and one little disc. Disc says three more please. SHATTER SHATTER SHATTER. Sounds Horsa killed street greenhouses. Stand still. All well – no alarm. Change disc twenty-seven more please. Very funny joke. Try back door and back door open!

HALLELUIA HORSA! In go. Up stairs. Right in bathroom. Big lump pink soap size breadloaf. Rosepink. Falseteethpink. One, two, three, four towels big, thick, hanging on fat hot copperypipes. Oh boy!

Horsa works taps, drops in plug. Bath (pale rosepink baby-pink, Mugstownpink) fills up up. Three jars salts green, yellow, lilac. Lilac favourite colour. Lielack.

Pour whole jar lielack in very hot bath and steamrise smells gardens heaven.

Offcome Horsa-boots. Hard work but off come. In time.

Off come black coat, trousers, jacket, waist-coats and let linings now unroll, telling tales of timegoneby. Plop. Dropping noises. Things falling off Horsa into deep hairy carpet. Some move fast. At a run. On various numbers of legs. They dash – not pausing to pass timeday.

All extras gone farewell. Horsa peels last newsprint and good scratch. Hasgo peeling newsprint footbottoms, but these old intelligences must soak. How is it boot in water-closet? It floats. Horsa's great big black left boot floats tasteful toilet like lobster (uncooked).

Beholdnow mirror. Amber-tinted-rose! And there (how he glares) is Horsa.

AND NOW –

Horsa mustersgether –

soap

flannels

back brushes

front brushes

sponges

nail brushes

sit there you lot

now then –

HERE COMES HORSA

In we go. Oh boy!

Maybe half-hour, maybe hour, maybe four hours. Best bath ever. Friends, let me say, let me proclaim –

PROCLAMATION
oh friends
THIS IS A REAL GOOD
BATH

When water goes off lovely boil have to twiddle butterflies. Golden butterflies, fat kind golden taps twiddle great big slab-elephant toes. OUCH! Get lost! Oh dear! No sense being burnt throwing back – brush. Mirror cracked now. Maybe yes, maybe no?

Maybe yes.

Hot water unending here – picked my house friends – hot water neverends like drizzle and mizzle and deluge and flood of wet night field-end somewhere down old green track. But HOT water, SOAPY water, on-on-ever, constant water. Just the ask. Just the twiddle.

Horsa how you spread!

How you swell in bathtub, how you rise in mound as tide washes steep pink shores.

Lotwater seems over bathroom carpet, soppingpink carpet. Pink carpet not very pink at present. Pink carpet black now where lielack water sops. Oh boy!

Horsa peers out over bathside. Horsa rests big nose-end on smoothpink bath-edge. Pink carpet not pink and now not carpet. More water-meadow. Flooded bog. Little movements in it occur and take place. Hereanthere. Some of Horsa's creepies drowning. Sad world.

Then down in again Horsa – slap, splursh. Deep, deep down in it.

So out gets last and hangs all towels allover Horsa – one round fatbelly, one round old shoulders, old soldiers, one round fine black headofhair, one last over all as second cover like tent. Tent with pink legs moves off down passage.

His room.

Kids room.

Her room.

Upagain – did Horsa turn off golden twiddleflies? – and what's this? Dad's room. Old Dad by look room full old stuff, boxes, rubbish, mess, hats. Dusgusting. Two big wardrobes.

Big fellow grandad. Wheregone not-here?

Maybe dead.

Maybe can't quite bring selves get rid old clothes.

Think nothing of it Missus. Can help there.

Big fellow grandad, same size Horsa. Good black suit, shirt, tie. Good boots too Horsa, getemonfeet. Ow! Grandad's toes not spread like Horsa's. Not gentlemanroad. Better get slit cut grandad's boots. Waitabit – here's good coat now – maybe hat.

Horsa hears rushing waters.

Horsa fancies hat.

Something for dark wet ditches.

Something for howling storm.

Bowler hat oh very nifty Horsa!

Pork-pie hat no not quite.

Whatsthisnow? Tall box!

TOP HAT!

Look-in-glass, lookinglass, Horsa. Good morning sir, and how do you do? Glory!

Oh boy!

Down again long landing and noise waters. Ah – new boots seem not let in landing waters. Landing stages landing waters and down kitchen get knife cut slit ease toe boot.

(What's new noise?)

Here's knife. Now then – whataboutit! Food. A foodstore and we have

ham,

  cheese,

    bread,

      tomato sauce,

        Suzie's sauce,

          Uncle's sauce,

            and

sweetie bics,

                pork pie (not hat)

                      pork pie juice sticky crust.

Bite pie, blow flakes, out of beard PUFF!

And here is cold dark stew on cold dark shelf.

Now then find bag (What noise again? Bell?) Nowthen Horsa takecare. Goslow. Put stew in paperbags. Don't get stew down nice new coat. What's fallen then eggs? All slippery. Crunch-crunch (Yes door bell – getopram). Dear me, long shelf full jars whole silly little cupboard comes way from wall. Red jam, orange jam, lumpy black-purple jam. Very pretty. Mind glass. Down go porridge plates unwashed off draining board, very sticky. But such tidy little Mugstown lady shoulda washed up. Now then –

Stew in pocket, sauce bottle otherpocket. Sausages where –

top hat TOP HAT! O.K. Horsa, bestgonow. Somebody out there front steps. Oh! Best crawlalong under housewall. Quiet now under steps. Grab pram.

Little cough, little twitter steps above. Lady ringing doorbell up above. Coming down steps.

'Excuse me? Hullo? Good morning? Is anybody there? I believe there are some old clothes for charity to be collected from this address. Excuse me sir, I wonder if you have anything for The Homeless?'

'Nothing about me, Ma'am, nothing about me.'

(Wurbly-burbly-gloshy-woshy-WAH)

'Eeeeeeeeeek!' screams good woman, 'Helphelp. Mad man!' Nobody notices. Goodbye friend.

Cat openseye. Smiles shuts it. 'Take your ease, Horsa.' What's Homeless?

Like cats.

And Horsa passes downstreet. Top hat (TOP HAT) full of sausages and pockets full of stew. Smell, smell the lielack as Horsa passes by. Shuffle, shuffle behind pram, shuffle under freezing trees. Grandad's leftboot bitight. Disremembered knife. Never mind find something soon. Maybe sell boots for real good used ones.

Now Horsa, get moveon. Openroad now boy. Loosen necktie, maybe chuckaway. In bin. Here's bin. Might find old sandwich. Good newspaper bin anyway – keep for later, Horsa. Back normal later. Horsa smells of lilac notforever. Paper padding needed soon as nights draw down. Monthortwo, yearortwo – Horsa no good telling time – but round beginningain. Thinking bath.

Hot day. Bath.

Water. Bath.

Bath. Etcetera.

Whileyetacourse – monthtwo, yeartwo, ('Evening officer, splendid day. Wurbly, burbly, gurgly –')

Yeartwoyet.

Smellsalielack.

Top hat full sausages. TOP HAT!

Great world.

Oh boy!

Lunch with Ruth Sykes

She was crying again last night and that made it easier for me this morning.

I said, 'I'm having lunch with Ruth Sykes today, dear.'

'Mmmm,' she said, black coffee one hand, toast the other, peering down at the morning paper laid all across the kitchen table – she never sits down at breakfast.

'So you'll be all right, dear?'

'Mmmm.'

'For lunch I mean – after surgery. I'll leave it ready in the oven. Just to take out.'

'What?'

'Your lunch, dear. After surgery. And your visits. It'll be in the oven.'

She looked at me through her big glasses – such a big, handsome daughter. How could such a great big woman have come out of me? I'm so small. Jack was small, too. And neither of us was anything much. Certaily nothing so clever as a doctor in either of the families, anywhere. It's funny – I look at her, my daughter, my Rosalind and I can't believe she's the same as the baby I had: the fat little round warm bright-eyed thing holding its wrists up in the pram against the light, carefully watching the leaves moving in the birch tree like a peaceful little fat cat. She's so bold and brave and strong now – fast car, doctor's bag slung in the back, stethoscope, white coat. So quick on the telephone. Oh it's wonderful to hear her on the telephone! – 'Yes? When was this? All right – do nothing until I'm there. I'll be with you in ten minutes.' Oh the lives she must save! She's a wonderful doctor.

But the crying is awful. It was really awful last night.

'Why can't you be here, mother?' (Flicks over page of *The Telegraph*. Peers closer.)

She never lets herself go even when she's happy. I think the last time I remember her being overwhelmed in any way by feeling happy was when she got into Oxford. And then she just opened the telegram and said, 'Oh my goodness!' and spilled a whole cup of coffee all down her school uniform – all over the clean floor.

'I'm having lunch with Ruth Sykes.'

She finished her coffee. ''Bye,' she says, 'Have a nice time. See you for supper – oh, no I won't. Forgot. I'll be at the hospital.'

'Till when, dear?'

'God – I don't know. Ten? Eleven?'

'All right, dear.'

The road outside as well as the front garden and the house is diminished without her. Energy has gone out of the morning.

I go back in the kitchen and start clearing up the breakfast. Am I *really* going? Dare I?

I wash things up and stand for a time looking at the china cupboard door before putting them away. I go upstairs and change into my dark blue wool suit and good shoes and stockings and look at my face in the glass.

It is a very silly face. Like an unintelligent bird. Birds are supposed to have intelligent faces, but I don't know. Mine is like a bird's but not a very bright bird. A C-stream bird. It's a timid self-conscious face. Ready to be made an ass of. An ass to be made of a bird. Rosalind does make me feel such an ass. She didn't as a baby – she used to get hold of bits of me then – my ear or my chin – and hang on tight, and laugh and laugh. It does seem a pity –.

Anyway I'm better looking than Ruth Sykes. I'm not an ass when I'm with Ruth Sykes either. I'm perfectly easy. We were at school together and she was nothing like so clever as I was though I was nothing special at all. I wish I *were* having lunch with Ruth Sykes.

I'm not though. I decided a fortnight ago and I'm not losing my nerve now. No I'm not.

Not with all the crying.

I'm going to London to see Michael.

95

*

The crying didn't start as soon as Michael stopped coming here. She was quite sane and calm and quiet at first, even rather nice to me. I remember she said would I like to go to the theatre with her once, and I got tickets for the two of us for *Rosenkavalier* – just locally. It's not my favourite at all and I expect she loathed it but we sat there together very friendly, side by side.

'Is Michael busy tonight?' – I hadn't realised then.

''Spect so,' she said.

She didn't stay in at home though, not at all. And she never mentioned him. She kept on being very nice to me for several weeks – sometimes she'd come and sit by me and watch the telly for a bit, and once I remember she said she liked my dress. Once she seemed to be looking at me as if she was going to say something and I just waited, I was so afraid of doing the wrong thing. I talk far too much you see. I'm a bit of a joke the way I talk once I get started.

She didn't say anything though and all I said after a day or two more was that Michael hadn't telephoned lately and were they going on holiday together again this summer. And she just got up and slammed out.

Then that night I heard her crying – awful, awful long sobs. They woke me up and I couldn't think whatever they were – like terrible sawing noises, seconds apart. I went out on the landing and they seemed to be coming from the top floor where she sleeps, and I went running up and stood outside her door.

Awful sobs.

Well, I daren't of course go in.

I went down again to my floor and back to bed with the door open and listened – just shaking, my eyes wide open, trying to imagine her face, all so smooth and assured, twisted up in the dark with the mouth crooked and those awful noises coming out of it.

Yet at breakfast she was just the same – coffee cup one hand, toast the other, peering down at the newspaper. Perhaps two lines had appeared above the nose, creased together, that was all.

'Sit down, dear. You'll strain your eyes.'

She didn't answer. I got up in a sudden rush and went all

round the table and I put my arm round her waist – she's so much taller than me – and I said. 'Darling, can't you sit down a minute?'

She said, 'Oh for Godssake, mother,' and pulled away.

I said, 'You'll hurt your eyes.'

'Is there any moment of the year,' she said, 'when you don't say that?'

'Do you think,' she said, 'that just once you could express a single original thought?'

I didn't hear her crying for a while and then three weeks ago it began again. For a week she was crying every single night. I got up each time. At first I walked round my room bumping things about. Then I took to going out on the landing and clicking on and off the light. Once I pulled the lavatory chain. The crying just went on. In the end – like last night – I took to going and sitting on the stairs outside her bedroom. It did no good of course, but it was all I could do and so I did it. I took the eiderdown and put it round me and I just sat there praying she would stop. Sometimes I told myself stories that she would come out and trip over me and say, 'Oh Mother!' and then I would hug her and hug her and say, 'Oh Rosalind, what happened? Tell me what happened. What *happened* to him?'

She never did.

The crying always stopped in the end – longer pauses between the sobs and then when the idiot birds began to wake up she'd be quiet at last. So funny. When she was a baby that was the time she would always wake up. She got a real nuisance about one and a half and I had to be quite firm. I used to go in and she'd be standing in her cot with her nappies round her ankles and her nightie all frills and her face like a rose.

'Now, Rosalind. Back to sleep. Too *soon*, baby. It's only five o'clock. The day hasn't started yet.' 'But the birds has begun to tweet,' she said. Oh she was lovely! 'The birds has begun to tweet.' And she wasn't two – still in nappies! I still tell that story, I'm ashamed to say. I oughtn't to because I know she hates it. She glares and stamps out or, even worse, she *withers* me with an icy stare. 'I wonder how many times Ruth Sykes has heard *that* story,' she says.

Well, I know I'm a fool.

Our doctor thought I was a fool all right a couple of weeks ago when I went to see him and said I had a bad heart and wanted to see a heart specialist. 'Well, well, Mrs Thessally,' he said. 'Shall I be the judge of that? What does your daughter say?'

'I haven't told her,' I said. 'I don't want her to know. But I am sure myself and I want to see a specialist. I want to see Dr Michael Kerr.'

'He's not the man I usually use. And anyway, let's have a look at you and see if we need to use anyone.'

He examined me and said he was glad to say that we need not use anyone. 'Perfectly normal heart it seems to me. Very good for your age. What are you – fifty? Fifty-two? No signs of trouble at all.'

But I went on and on at him. I do rather go on and on when I am not with Rosalind and then I hardly speak.

'Look, my dear – I can't send you up to Harley Street with absolutely nothing wrong with you,' he said.

'My daughter says that three-quarters of the people she sees have absolutely noghing wrong with them. It's all in their minds. This is my mind,' I said. 'I can't get it out of my mind.'

'Not sleeping?' he said.

'No.' (That was true anyway.)

'Eating?'

'Not much.'

'Something worrying you?' he said, putting his finger-tips together and looking over them like an advertisement for medical insurance. Whatever use in the world would it be to tell him.

'My heart,' I said at last. 'I know I'm being a fool.' I have big blue eyes. As a matter of fact I notice that if I look at people steadily with my eyes open wide and think very honestly of what I have just said they often smile at me as if I had given pleasure. The doctor did now.

'*All* right,' he said undoing his finger tips. 'We'll give you a letter for Doctor Michael Kerr and make an appointment.'

I had it in my handbag now and I carried my handbag with great care as I went to the tube station and took the train to

Oxford Circus. I had a hat on and good gloves and pearl studs in my ears though only Woolworths. I walked to Michael's nursing home calm as calm and one or two people – one of them a tall black man with a lovely smile – noticed me and I smiled back, particularly at the black man who looked kind.

I didn't feel so good in the hospital though. There was a dreadful woman behind the reception desk. 'For Dr *Kerr*?' she said and looked at me as if nobody as insignificant as me had a right to see Michael. 'Are you Private?'

'No. Not really,' I said. 'But I am today.'

'I'm sorry. I don't understand.'

'I'm National Health but I didn't think it was right to see Dr Kerr on the National Health because my doctor doesn't think there's anything wrong with me. So I insisted on paying.'

Up shot her neat, pencilled eyebrows. '*I see*,' she said (another nutter). 'Will you sit over there and wait please?'

She took my letter and opened it and smoothed it out and pinned it on a board and read it. Had she the right to do that? I must ask Rosalind.

But this was something I couldn't ask Rosalind. This was very private. Rosalind would never know. I was Private today all right.

The receptionist looked closely at me now and then with gleaming eyes, and I tried to look at other things. I looked at two doors marked MALES and FEMALES. They had been newly painted over. You could still just see where LADIES and GENTLEMEN had been. 'Males' and 'females' looked dreadful somehow. Like a zoo.

I have always dreaded and hated hospitals though Rosalind of course doesn't know. I kept looking at the notices and thinking 'This is why', though I couldn't begin to tell you what I meant.

'Would you come this way please, Mrs Thessally?' – a nice, frizzy nurse as fat as Rosalind was when she was a baby, took me along to a waiting room and then after a minute another pure, thin Chinese nurse came out of a door and held it open and said, 'Come in, Mrs Thessally.'

I tried to get up but was unable to move.

'This way, Mrs Thessally.'

Still I sat.

She came across and said, 'Come along, Mrs Thessally. Dr Kerr doesn't bite,' and laughed showing little neat teeth.

And there I was sitting in front of a desk the size of a tennis court and there behind it sat Michael who used to be always having supper with us, making funny faces at me through the kitchen window as he came round by the back door, making me drop the teapot. Weeding the garden for me, looking at his watch and saying 'Where *is* the woman? Why does your daughter work so hard? Why isn't she coming to play tennis?' Two years and more Michael had been in our lives.

He looked older, grimmer and even bigger in his white coat. He had glasses – that was new – and he was reading my notes with the same drawn-down expression Rosalind has now.

'Now then,' he said, 'Mrs – er?'

I sat.

'Mrs *Thessally*!' he said.

And I sat looking at my hands in the good gloves. I didn't look at him any more. All that I needed to know I knew. I knew it from the horrified, upward-rising inflection of his voice. 'Mrs *Thessally*.'

And there on the table was the note from my own doctor saying that there was nothing wrong with me but that I had insisted on seeing him and only him.

I knew there and then how terribly I had blundered. And, as with Rosalind and as never before with dear Michael, I was quite unable to speak.

A nurse creature came in and said, 'So sorry, doctor – could you just sign these,' and he did. She went out. He moved the ashtray and things on the tennis court about and cleared his throat. I could hear the small tick of the little gold clock on the shelf behind him – one of Rosalind's birthday presents.

The door burst open behind and someone called, 'Oh sorry – could I have a quick word?' and a young, carefree-looking houseman came in with coat and stethoscope flapping. 'I say, Mrs Arnold's doing well.'

Michael said, 'Oh yes.'

'Marvellous. She could go out today, I'd think.'

'You wouldn't think if you'd seen her last night. She collapsed.'

'What!'

'Yes. We were with her two hours.'

'Oh God. Nobody told me.'

'Then it's just as well you saw me, isn't it? I hope you haven't told her?'

'What?'

'That she can go home today.'

'No. No.'

'She needs a good bit of care.'

The houseman vanished and the door closed.

Michael got up and went and stood looking out of the window and I got up, too.

'I'd better go,' I said. He said nothing. I got to the door and I just had to look round at him and there was his familiar shape made so godlike and all-powerful by its setting, larger than life, so different from when it used to be crawling in and out of my delphiniums setting slug-pellets and calling down curses on my absent, over-working, non-tennis-loving daughter. Oh, however had I dared!

'Mrs T,' he said to the distant chimney pots of Bayswater, 'this is absolutely none of my doing. I want you to know. Nothing at all can come from me. I think that since Rosalind clearly hasn't told you then I should. It is very much all over.'

'Female,' I said.

'What?' he said turning round.

'Female.' I was thinking of the awful notices on the door outside. I don't know that I really knew what I was talking about but I went on. 'She couldn't come to you, you know. I know all the equality and things, and she does seem to be so completely a doctor. But there are still very deep conventions.'

He frowned and swung away and looked out of the window again.

'There are things a woman can't do. It's so odd – but she can't. Unless she's a man-woman. It has nothing to do with status, Women's Lib and so on. It is an instinct. Rosalind would never, never write or ring you up – unless for a death or something. She would let all you have had together go before –'

And I was gone, out of the room, out of the waiting room, out of the hospital, back into Oxford Street and my heart was beating so loud it was probably making more noise than Mrs

Arnold's who'd collapsed. I seemed to be crying, too. I walked the whole length of Oxford Street looking in all the shop-windows and what was in them all I don't know. When I got to Tottenham Court Road there was a huge cinema and I bought a ticket and went in. It seemed to be a film made for giants. The screen was so big you had to turn your head to get it all in. Enormous people came bounding out of it at you, singing at the top of their voices – happy children – nuns who became governesses and married princes and escaped from the Germans and sang and sang and sang. What curious lives people lead.

There were very few people in the cinema – an old woman in my row was fast asleep and the only other person was a greasy young man with his feet up on the seat in front who kept on getting up and going back to buy ice-creams. At the end of the film when there seemed to be some sort of a royal wedding going on I got up and went out and found it was quite dark; and I thought I would look for a cup of tea.

But I walked all down Bloomsbury Way without finding one and at the end of it I found I was standing instead on the steps of an hotel.

It was a very busy, ugly-looking hotel with a lot of students sitting about in the foyer with haversacks and the carpets very threadbare and not clean, and without knowing what on earth I was about to do I pulled the glass doors open and went in and booked a room for the night. It was six pounds in advance and I paid out of my purse, and went upstairs. I lay on the bed which was narrow and hard and looked at the ceiling. 'What is the good of it? Suffering like this for her,' I thought, and I was so tired I hadn't even taken off my shoes – 'After all,' I thought, 'it isn't me.'

I must have fallen asleep then because it was suddenly very still, and from something in the silence and the blackness of the window it was obviously the middle of the night. I sat up and felt frightened and dazed for a moment, until I remembered where I was. Then I found that my thoughts had not moved on though my watch said three a.m. I was still saying, 'Why suffer so? It's not me. It's not my affair.'

I began to think in a way I had never thought before in all Rosalind's twenty-seven years. I thought of the breakfasts when she never looked in my direction; the months and months and months when she was only a hurried figure appearing for meals, retiring to her study, rushing out to see to others; of all the years when – except for Ruth Sykes and Mrs Somebody in the road or Uncle James at Hastings, because we've so few relatives and since Jack died I've not had much interest in friends and going about – all the years when every telephone call and letter and message and enquiry and invitation has always been for her. I thought of her great big handsome face that never smiles at mine, the way she winces whenever I open my mouth, the way she so clearly despises me. Of how the only times she had ever softened at all into the Rosalind of long ago and before Jack died was when Michael was there – and she had never actually *invited* Michael, now I came to think of it. He had found his own way to us, first just dropping her at the gate, or picking her up, usually too early for her. 'Oh Lord! Sorry,' she had always said, bursting in on us as we sat together talking or Michael weaving about, looking under saucepan lids in the kitchen. 'It's all right,' he'd say. 'Your Mama and I have been enjoying ourselves.' I remembered the slight surprise I had seen in her face sometimes at this remark – the frequent quick look at me to see what I was wearing and relief if it was something she didn't think ghastly.

As the dawn began to make the sky grow pale and dirty over Bloomsbury, I realised that after all I didn't like Rosalind very much.

And as I fell asleep and the local sparrows began to tweet I said clearly and out loud, 'I have had enough. Oh, I have had enough.'

When I woke about half past nine I washed in the nasty little basin, but only my face and hands and not with any real interest and, still just in the same wool suit I had slept in, I went downstairs and I sat for a time in the foyer. There were more students about than ever, getting hot drinks in paper cups out of a machine on the wall. I felt out of place in my hat and gloves and pearl studs and rather faint in all the bustle and heat. A gingerish little girl of about eighteen or nineteen flopped down on the seat beside me and began to read a map of London. She knocked my arm. 'Oh, I'm sorry,' she said. 'Oh! – are you all right?' –

'If I gave you the money,' I said, 'could you get me a cup of tea out of the machine?'

She got it and came and stood over me while I drank it, with a serious, earnest face. '*Are* you all right?' she said. 'Shall I get someone?'

She asked like a child asking someone wiser. 'No, dear,' I said. 'Thanks so much though.' A funny, ordinary little thing. The sort I might have had. The sort really you'd expect Jack and me to have had. The sort I wish –.

I went out into Bloomsbury Way and into Museum Street and thought I might go to the British Museum, but the street looked very long and I didn't seem to make any great progress down it. I felt really most odd. 'I shall buy a present for that poor Mrs Arnold,' I said to someone passing, who looked alarmed. A bus passed very close to me at some lights. I felt the wind of it. It blew my skirt against me. A taxi driver yelled at me as I just made the kerb. I thought, 'I suppose I should really be more careful and perhaps I should move on now?'

What I meant by move on was left for my subsconscious to decide and I was pleased that it did, relieving me of responsibility. It directed me to Russell Square tube station and suggested that I descend. I changed, or I supposed I changed, at a couple of stations because in an unspecified time – an hour or a day – I found that the train had stopped at Putney Bridge. I was home it seemed. I got out.

Now our house is in one of those streets to the right of Putney High Street and a long walk from either Putney Bridge or the High Street Station. Even a bus doesn't take you very near. You have to get across the High Street, too, at the outset, and that isn't nothing on a Saturday morning. 'Look alive,' someone shouted as I dithered on an island. I made the further shore and trudged on. I trudged down Lacey Road and Cawnpore Terrace. On I trudged past all the plum and purple houses, row upon row with names like Quantox and East Lynne. Jack was so fond of Putney. I've never liked it much.

Perhaps I'll move. I'll just go away. Well, really, it's very silly just waiting hand and foot on a great twenty-seven-year-old woman you don't like and who doesn't like you.

The elastic went in my locknits. I've always worn locknits – briefs and loose legs are not nice in anyone my age and I like a gusset. They have the old-fashioned elastic which you can still get at the Home and Colonial, very reliable and long-lasting whatever Rosalind says. Never before in all the years has the elastic broken and the knicker-leg begun to fall.

Then I turned into our road and I saw the police car.

And I ran.

I ran past Mrs Fergusson at number 63 though she was waving her arms about and calling, and Mrs Atkinson next door was calling too, standing in her front garden and looking over at our house. It didn't seem like our road at all somehow. Very lively it seemed. And myself at the centre of things – my knicker leg hanging.

Then a policeman came out of our house and Michael with him, talking together. And then I knew. There and then at once I knew.

She had killed herself.

She had cried last night and come out of her room to the bathroom and got all the aspirins and killed herself. The one night I had not been on the landing waiting, the one night in all her life I had abandoned her and ceased to care. A suicide note. Michael's name on the envelope. Michael summoned to the house by the police.

And then I was lying flat on my back on my own sitting-room sofa with three faces loking down at me – one I had not seen before, a policeman's, very young and sensible. One was Michael's face and one – Oh God, oh God, oh God be thanked! – was Rosalind's!

And her face was all wet and streaming all round and under the glasses and she seemed to be shouting in a fierce and furious way – yelling, yelling 'Where were you? Where were you? How could you?'

The policeman shook hands with Michael who saw him I suppose to the door while Rosalind's maniac yelling went on. 'We thought you were dead. We thought you were dead. Under a car –'

Michael came in and got her by the shoulders and shook her.

'Shut up at once and go and get your mother some tea. 'Sobbing like a great booby she went and I sat up and Michael and I looked at each other.

'Oh Michael, I'm so sorry. I shouldn't have. I shouldn't have interfered. It was nothing to do with me. I don't know what I was thinking –'

'Hush,' he said. He sat down on a stool and took my hand and we sat quiet.

'I rang Ruth Sykes. Don't pretend you were with Ruth Sykes,' Rosalind cried hurtling in with a milk jug. 'Out of our minds with – Oh! Good heavens! Knicker *leg*!' she shrieked. She disappeared and there was a great noise of crockery crashing in the kitchen.

'Oh dear,' I said. 'She's so hopeless. I'd better go –'

'Hush,' he said.

'She rang,' he said, 'she rang this morning.'

'So I was even wrong about that.'

'No,' he said, 'she left a message. She said "It is my mother. It is a matter of life and death". You said "only if it were a death".'

'Well, it wasn't,' I said.

'From the look of you at the moment it might have been.'

'Oh Michael. I'm sorry. I didn't want to make you feel you had to come running –'

'I didn't. I decided yesterday I'd come back. After you'd gone. They caught me leaving for here after she'd rung off. I was leaving when she phoned but she doesn't know that. She said, "Oh how quick you've been", when she opened the door. I felt – not commendable.'

I closed my eyes, for it was all too difficult. Then in flew Rosalind again with a tray of oddments – the old brown tea-pot and three stray cups. She'd taken off her glasses and her hair was falling down and her cheeks were bright pink right up close under the eyes, all roses like a child again. She really is a lovely girl.

'How could you,' she was still crying out. 'Out of my mind – You've never, ever – Whenever did you – ?' and so on. Michael stretched up his other hand and took hers and said 'Hush,' again, 'Let your poor mother rest.' He said, 'I've never met such

106

an emotional pair. If you don't both stop I'll have to call a doctor.'

'Oh don't try to be funny, Michael.' But, 'Hush,' he said again. 'Your poor Mama is going to need all the strength she's got to organise this wedding.'

And Rosalind poured a whole cup of tea all down the front of her dress and onto the floor and dropped the cup and smashed it (the last of the Worcester) and she just gazed at him.

'It beats me,' he said – but gazing back at her with such joy – 'It beats me. Medically,' he said, 'Genetically' (and I shall tell Ruth Sykes) 'it beats me how such an intelligent woman could produce such a stupid great child.'

Dossie

'Well, of course there's Dossie.'

'Who's Dossie?'

'Well, Dossie. Auntie Dossie. She used to send you Christmas presents.'

'I don't remember any Dossie.'

'Well maybe they were only cards. Your father's sister.'

'I've never heard of her,' said Dorothea.

Her mother scuffled about in a drawer and then in an address book.

'Does she live in London?'

'Yes. Ah – here we are. In Lower Sloane Street, S.W.3. That sounds central. I'd say that was quite central. Where's the Heart Hospital?'

'W.C. somewhere.'

'Well then. *Well* then! Auntie Dossie.'

'She doesn't know me. She's never seen me. We can't just ring and ask –'

'Whyever not? I'll write. It won't be for long. It'll only be for one night. You stay with Lucy Whatsname the whole week before. It's just the night before the operation she can't have you. They'll have you with him the night after if it's necessary. And after that if you need –. If they need –. If you prefer it to going back to Lucy round the corner. I'll write. I'll write now to Dossie.'

'But whoever is she? Why haven't I met her? Have you ever met her?'

'No. He never bothered. Your father never bothered with his relations.'

'But his own sister!'

'I wasn't approved,' said her mother. 'I was the disaster.

Married him before he qualified. Then he stopped trying to qualify and then he died. It was all said to be my fault. I'm no mixer. Anyway they were rich.'

'You'll do no such thing,' said James. 'You'll go to a good hotel.' His fingers were thin as an old man's fingers as he moved papers on the desk, jerkily, as if a list of good hotels in London lay somewhere about waiting consultation.

'We can't afford a hotel. In London. The train fare's bad enough. You know what hotels cost here. What they can be in London –. No – I'll go to this Dossie.'

So on the last day of the week James had spent in hospital preparing for the operation, Dorothea brought her suitcase and was allowed to leave it by the porter's desk while she was with him in the ward, and at the end of the afternoon, when she had said goodbye to him, she came down and picked it up again and set off to find Lower Sloane Street. In the clattery old lift at Russell Square tube station it came to her that tomorrow James would die.

The big, good-looking Sister she had grown to know quite well during the week had caught her half an hour ago as she left the ward and asked if she had time to come for a little talk with Mr Barnsley. She had thought, Barnsley? Something to do with Welfare? – then remembered, as the Sister put an arm on her shoulder and ushered her in to the presence that of course, Mr Barnsley was the surgeon.

He was a big bony noisy jumpy man spinning about in a revolving chair behind a wide desk. He jumped up. He settled her down, offered a cigarette, a drink. Like James he shuffled papers as he talked, and the talk was the antithesis of the cheery, jerky, physical image of the good-tempered, extrovert dashing young doctor. From the pleasant mouth came words that meant that James was very likely going to die. As James himself had been told, without the operation he would certainly die. Within the year. So that the operation was of course inevitable. No choice. It made it much easier for them all that there was no choice. And it was a fine operation, a great chance. This had all been discussed weeks ago, had it not?

But she did realise, didn't she? The operation was also very

109

serious. Yes. James's condition was very serious. The chances about forty-sixty Mr Barnsley would say. Yes. Forty-sixty.

There were children? Oh yes – of course there were children. He remembered now. Being looked after by a granny. Where would we be without grannies? Good. And accommodation – that had been seen to? London a very different place from Lancashire – sorry Leicestershire. Always mixed them up. Hope the hospital had given all assistance? Ah – a friend. A friend living just round the corner. What luck. And tonight, an aunt. How lucky these days to have an aunt. He, Mr Barnsley, had no aunts. He had found this a loss. Blood is thicker than water on these –.

Catching Dorothea's eye he did not develop this theme but spun round in his chair and wiped a clean patch of window cleaner. Then he spun back.

'What time is the operation?'

'In the afternoon. Above five o'clock.'

'What time should I be here? Could I come in again in the morning?'

'No, we don't like that very much. The patient should rest in the morning. You've said –. You've seen him just now?'

'Yes.'

'Then best to see him again when it's all over.'

He came round the desk and shook hands with her. Again the arm along the shoulders. 'Great athlete, wasn't he? Fearful bad luck. Very young. What's the book?'

'It's the new P. D. James. A thriller. He's just given it to me. I adore her. It's to take my mind –. A surprise –' Weakness and terror made her face sneer.

'*That's* the style,' said the surgeon. 'That's the way. Do you want something to make you sleep? Right. Then off you go to the good aunt.'

And he had timed it perfectly she thought at Bond Street, the coming round the desk, the handshake, the patting of the shoulder, the easing to the door. A routine, A dance. At Oxford Circus she could think of nothing but the surgeon's hand upon the desk, upon the window. At Victoria she thought, no choice – much easier – essential. Then coming up the steps of Sloane Square tube station she thought blindlingly only of James –

James himself, not James in relation to herself or as any part of his children, not working, not drinking, not sailing, not laughing, not playing tennis, not being the chap everybody liked, but James within his own self, the self separate as it had been from the beginning before she was born: the unchanging eyes of the old photographs, the particular private self looking out of a pram, looking up from sandcastles, chin raised, four square to the world, brave, a winner. And inside him the heart that hadn't squared up to the rest. 'A Friday night heart,' he called it, 'a knocking-off-time heart. A heart God passed in a hurry. A down-tools and off to the local heart,' James said, 'and my word don't I wish I was off to the local tonight.'

After leaving the surgeon Dorothea did not look back at the hospital. She thought, now he is on his own, separate. It's a freedom. It has nearly started now like a birth. Soon it will be better. It is almost as if he has got health. I am sick. It is I who am ill. I am crying for myself, not for him. These are tears for my own trouble – James can cope. He's in other people's hands. I am allowed tears. I will parade them. I need help tonight and I will cry.

I am the one, she said to the wax figures in Peter Jones's windows, cherished with clothes and necklaces, I am the one who needs help and love tonight.

She found she had walked almost the length of the King's Road and turned down Oakley Street to the river and a phone box. She phoned Leicester and talked to both the children. Miles said, 'It's Mummy. Have you got my Action Man?' Emily said, 'But you rang only a minute ago.'

'I didn't. It was after tea. Have you done your homework?'

'It's been Doctor Who. It's Thursday.'

'Oh. Yes. Can I speak to Granny?'

'She's doing the supper.'

'Well, get her.'

'What is it?' – breathless voice, hands just dried at the sink. 'Is anything? Has something? You've only just rung.'

'No, It's all right. Just to say he's all right.'

'Where are you?' Sharp, wretched.

'By the river somewhere.'

'Oh dear, is it S.W.3?'

'I don't know. I've got an A to Z. I'll find it.'

'Have you had anything to eat?'

'I had some lunch.'

'But it's eight o'clock. After. You must go. You must go to Dossie.'

'Did she say to be there for supper?'

'Well, no. But of course she meant you to be there for supper.'

'All right.'

'Dorothea?'

'Yes?'

'Do go to Dossie, dearie. I mean, she's a relative.'

'I – don't know what that means.'

'Dorothea? Are you all right? Look, I'll telephone Dossie.'

'No. I'll go. I'm all right.'

'I mean – what are families for?'

'Yes.'

'I mean, she's probably frantic – waiting for you. I told her you know. She knows all about it. She'll be keeping something hot.'

'Something hot?'

'Yes.'

'I don't – I'd –'

'What?'

'I don't think they do. Keep things hot. In London.'

'But you're a relation.'

'I don't think they have them.'

'Don't be ridiculous. Now go there. Dorothea. Promise.'

She walked along the Chelsea Embankment to the bridge. She kept the book under her coat. Under her shirt. She walked all the way along the Royal Hospital Road and stood looking at the cannon. Men as old and frail as shadows moved behind the windows. A gem of a man with white waxed moustachios and wearing scarlet and gold strutted by and in through the gates – eighty if a day. Dorothea looking through his glowing uniform and his woollen underclothing through his skin and his bones and his rib-cage to his steadily thumping heart. Useless, useless useless old man, fit as a knife.

She walked to the crossroads that led to Pimlico and saw that

112

one of them was labelled Lower Sloane Street and she walked up it. In the bastion of hideous plum and black brick she found a house with Dossie's number painted upon a brick, painted yellow. There were five steps up, each with canary-yellow line painted along its edge to avoid falls. The bell-pull was brass and polished. All the houses round about had a panel of bells, sometimes ten, but Auntie Dossie still lived in a whole house. Dossie was still rich.

She rang.

No sound, no movement, no flicker of light.

She walked down the steps again and looked up. The whole great brutal house was in darkness. Above it and below it on the street the other flat-filled houses were lit. Music came from one of them. From next door a group of people came out in a rush, eating hamburgers, talking and calling. A boy in an embroidered jacket and jeans and one earring carried a guitar. Remote as summer he looked at Dorothea.

She climbed the steps and rang again. She is my aunt, she thought, the sister of my father. It is only for tonight. I won't even talk about it. She stood the overnight case on the top step and found that the glass panels in the front door swayed about a little. She thought, it's only hunger. It seemed a long time ago that she had felt she had a right to display tears.

She had not in fact had any lunch. She had left the hospital for only a quarter of an hour all day to go shopping for things James needed – more soap, tissues, squash – and she had had no breakfast. Lucy did not eat breakfast and had had to be off to work by eight. Her boy-friend had been expected at the flat tonight – would be there now. From Paris. Lucy had been all awry this morning trying to think how she could buy and cook the dinner in time, choose the wine and – honestly it's not as if he was just anyone, Dorothea. Honestly, I'd have put anyone else off. (Unless she was making it all up – not being able to stand tonight. Feeling that if there were an aunt –)

Her mother had said that of course Dossie had expected her for supper. It was a bit late. But there'd be something. She rang again. And far away in the depths of Lower Sloane Street a light was switched on and slow steps approached the door and a head looked round it, a fat, smiley, old-woman-little-girl head, decorated with careful hair, earrings, round blue eyes. The door opened.

'Dorothea.'

As kind as could be.

'Come in. Well. How are you?'

'I'm –'

'Just put the little case down in the hall and come in.'

She shuffled on puffy ankles to a room overcrowded with cushions and brass. Too many sofas, too many rugs. Some great dead animal skin collapsed on the floor, walls covered with portraits of long-dead, keen-eyed men, medals aglow. A little fat living man sat in one of the largest armchairs. He had a round red mouth and crossed-over legs. He did not get up.

'Here's Uncle Weejer,' said Auntie Dossie. 'Here's Dorothea.'

The man blew a little air from behind his lips, recrossed his legs and nodded and pressed a button on the chair arm. An enormous television set sprang into life. 'We'll just watch the news,' said Auntie Dossie, 'and then we'll have a drink.'

Dorothea watched the Prime Minister making a stern statement to the unions. Then she watched a union leader making a stern statement to the nation. Then she watched an African leader making a stern statment to another African leader, and then she watched the Queen in a pink coat and hat waving with resignation and authority at a group of children hanging over a rope. Then she watched some small, rare animals born successfully into a zoo, their hearts beating visibly and strongly under new fur. Then she watched a man with a very friendly face tell her that tomorrow would be fine but with showery spells.

'Now,' said Auntie Dossie.

'Sunny spells and showers,' said the fat man.

'Now for a drink. Come with me, dear.'

Dorothea and Dossie descended to the kitchen.

'Tea. Coffee or cocoa?' asked Dossie. 'We always have a drink before we go to bed.'

Holding a chair Dorothea said, 'Oh – cocoa,' and Dossie padded from stove to tap to fill a big kettle with cold water. 'It will do for bottles too.'

'Bottles?'

'Uncle and I always have a hot bottle.'

'Oh. Yes.'

'Now tell me, dear, how are you enjoying London?'

'My husband –'

'Rowntree or Cadbury?'

'Oh – I don't suppose –'

'Yes, dear?'

'I don't suppose I could have a piece of bread?'

'Bread, dear?'

'Yes. Just a little – bread.'

'Oh, I think so. I think –' She prowled about.

'Your mother is well?'

'Yes.'

'Ah.'

They stood a long time watching the kettle. Dossie said, 'Such a pity – your mother –' Some time later but before there was a sign of steam she tremblingly began to fill a cup, which had a small teaspoonful of cocoa powder in the bottom, with water.

'There's a little milk,' she said. 'In the pantry I think.'

'I'll find it,' said Dorothea. In the pantry stood a big steak pie with only a third of it gone, a slab of cheese and a dish of fruit. 'And the husband is improving all the time?' said Dossie, following her in.

'Well, as a matter of fact –'

'Good. There's the milk dear. In the blue tin. Stir it in well. Now somewhere there just might be a Marie biscuit.'

'If there were a little – bread?'

'Oh – bread,' said Dossie.

For a while they watched the iron kettle again. It was still not singing. Dossie held the empty water bottles to her stomach. On the draining board stood the unwashed dishes of what had been the pie and something like a good fruit fool. There was a number of dirty saucepans. 'So little help now,' said Dossie. 'Your uncle and I have never got used –'

Dorothea heard herself offering to do the washing up.

'That would be kind, dear.'

Dorothea washed up in warmish water into which Dossie poured a careful extra trickle from the kettle. She showed

Dorothea where to put everything away. 'Could you fill the bottles, dear. My poor old wrists –'

'And now for bed. Come along, Weejer.'

They went upstairs all together, Dorothea last. Uncle and aunt clutched water-bottle bouquets at their bedroom doors.

'Your bedroom's up the next flight again. I think the bed's made up. I can't come up because of my poor ankles, but it's a nice room. Have you all you want?'

As she started up to the bedroom the uncle pushed air through his lips again. 'Washing,' he said. 'Bathroom no heat. Often undress there though. Open airing-cupboard door. Don't want pneumonia. Can't do with sickness.'

'Thank you.'

He was still standing at his door as she came down again with her sponge bag. 'Better tomorrow,' he said.

She felt a great blush of gratitude, a prick of tears.

'Very hopeful. Very hopeful they were. Though I trust the other channel more. Can spot a trough of dirty weather a hundred miles off.'

She left at eight. Auntie Dossie in a fluffy dressing gown again stood watching the kettle. 'Won't you wait for a cup of tea?' she said. 'It won't be long. Just a bag in a cup? Well never mind. It's been very nice to meet you. I hope you have a really encouraging day.'

At the front door it seemed as if the BBC team had been wrong, for the rain soaked down. A shining, sopping queue of people stood at the bus-stop opposite. Umbrellas butted, feet set up splashes, cars cut cold showers of spray, macintoshes clung. Dorothea unbuttoned her coat to put her book inside. She said, 'Thank you for having me to stay.'

'Well, we've quite enjoyed it,' Dossie said. 'After all – my brother –. We were brought up in my generation to believe in the family you know.' She let the thought go and stopped, utterly blank. She seemed to be listening for something. 'Goodbye,' she said and almost pushed Dorothea out of the house. The book fell and Dorothea picked it up.

'Well I never!' said Dossie, 'The new one. Oh, your uncle and I do love P. D. James!'

She shall not, she shall not, she shall not, by *God* she shall not – Dorothea clung tight to the book and at the same moment recognised what she had seen a moment before in Dossie's face – the listening blankness. 'It is fear,' she thought. 'It's just age and fear. She doesn't feel strong enough to hear –!'

'Oh thank you, How very kind!' said Dossie. 'We love a thriller.'

On the bottom step Dorothea in the rain looked back. Dossie's little silly head bobbed and smiling above the book and Dorothea began to laugh. 'Enjoy it,' she said – and, 'Wait till I tell him,' she thought. 'They even got his present. His last present. Just wait – he'll laugh. Oh, he'll die!'

And, 'No, he won't, she decided. Quite certainly she knew then that he would not.

'Goodbye,' she called – 'Oh and by the way, I might be back tonight. Late. So could you keep me some supper?' and she laughed several times as she splashed along, turning her face blithely to the hard weather.

A Spot Of Gothic

I was whizzing along the road out of Wensleydale through Low Thwaite beyond Naresby when I suddenly saw a woman at her cottage gate, waving at me gently like an old friend. In a lonely dale this is not very surprising, as I had found out. Several times I have met someone at a lane end flapping a letter that has missed the post in Kirby Thore or Hawes. 'It's me sister's birthday tomorrow. I near forgot' or 'It's the bill fort telephone. We'll be cut off next thing.' The curious thing about this figure, so still and watchful, was that it was standing there waving to me in the middle of the night.

It was full moon. I had been out to dinner at Mealbeck. I had only been living in the North for two months and for one month alone. I had joined my husband near Catterick camp the minute he had found us a house, which was only a few days before he found that the regiment was being posted to Hong Kong. The house he had found was beautiful, old and tall in an old garden, on the edge of a village on the edge of the fell. It was comfortable and dark with a flagged floor and old furniture. Roses and honeysuckle were nearly strangling black hedges of neglected yew. There was nice work to be done.

It was the best army house we had ever found. The posting to Honk Kong promised to be a short one. I had been there before and hated it – I hate crowded places – and I decided to stay behind alone.

He said, 'But you will be alone, mind. The camp is a good way off and most people will have gone with us. It's the North. You'll make no friends. They take ten years to do more than wag their heads at you in the street up here. Now, are you sure?'

I said I was and I stayed and found that he was quite wrong. Within days, almost within hours of my miserable drive home from Darlington Station to see him off, I found that I was behaving as if I'd always known the people here and they were doing the same to me. I got home from the station and stopped the car outside my beautiful front door and sat still, thinking, 'He has gone again. Again he has gone. What a marriage. Always alone. Shall I forget his face again? Like last time? Shall I begin to brood? Over-eat? Drink by myself in the evenings – rather more every evening? Shall I start tramping about the lanes pretending I like long walks?' I sat there thinking and a great truculent female head with glaring eyes stuck itself through the car window.

'D'you want some *beans*?'

'Oh!'

'Some *beans*? Stick beans?'

'Oh I don't –? Can you spare –?'

'Beans, beans. Masses of beans. They're growin' out of me ears. Grand beans. Up to you.'

'I'd love some beans.'

A sheaf of them was dumped on the seat beside me. 'There's plenty more. You've just to say. So 'e's off then? The Captain?'

'Yes.'

'Well, yer not to fret. There's always a cup of tea at our place. Come rount back but wear yer wellies or you'll get in a slather int yard.'

In the post office they asked kindly for news. Of how I was settling, of where I had come from. The vicar called. A man in a land-rover with a kind face – the doctor – waved his hat. A woman in the ironmonger's buying paraffin in gloves and a hat invited me to tea in a farmhouse the size of a mill with a ha-ha and a terrace at the back, gravel a foot thick and a thousand dahlias stalked like artillerymen and luminious with autumn. The tea cups must have been two hundred years old.

I was asked to small places too – a farm so isolated that the sheep and cows looked up aghast when I found my way to it, and the sheep-dogs nearly garrotted themselves on the end of hairy ropes.

'You'll be missin the Captain,' the farmer's wife said as she opened the door. Her accent was not the local one.

I said, 'You talk differently,' and she said, 'Well, I would do. I

119

come from Stennersceugh. It was a Danish settlement long since. It's all of ten miles off.'

Never mind in my life had I had so much attention paid to me by strangers, nor been told so many intimate things from the heart – of marriages, love and death; of children or the lack of them, fears of sickness, pregnancy; of lost loves and desperate remedies. Three old ladies living by the church, I heard, drank three crates of sherry a week ('It's the chemist delivers'). A husband had 'drowned 'isself in Ash Beck for fear of a thing growing out of the side of his head'.

There seemed to be total classlessness, total acceptance, offence only taken if you gave yourself airs, offered money in return for presents or didn't open your door wide enough at the sound of every bell. There was a certain amount of derision at bad management – 'She never gets out to the shops till twelve o'clock.' 'She hasn't had them curtains down in a twelve-month' – but I met no violence, no hatred. There were threats of 'bringin' me gun' to walkers on the fells with unleashed dogs, but not one farmer in ten possessed a gun or would have known how to use if he had. Language addressed to animals was foul and unrefined, ringing over the fells and sheep dips and clipping sheds – but bore no relation to conversation with humans or at any rate not with me. 'Come ere yer bloody, buggerin little – 'ello there, Mrs Bainbridge, now. Grand day. Comin over for yer tea then?'

Alan had told me that when he came home I'd be used to my tea as my supper and then more tea just before bedtime and I would forget how to cook a steak. However he was wrong again, because it had been dinner I had been invited to at Mealbeck the night of the waving woman, and a much better dinner than I'd ever have got in Aldershot.

Mealbeck is the big Gothic house of two sisters – a magnificent cold, turretted, slightly idiotic house, something between the Brighton Pavilion and the Carpathians. We ate not in a corner of it but the corner of a corner, passing from the tremendous door, over flagged halls, a great polar-bear skin rug and down a long cold passage. At the end was a little room which must once have been the housekeeper's and crammed into it among the housekeeper's possessions – a clock, a set of bells, a little hat-stand, a photograph of servants like rows of suet dumplings, starched and stalwart and long ago dead – were a Thomas Lawrence, photographs by Lenare and haunted Ypres faces in 1914 khaki. On the housekeeper's old table where she must have handed out the wages were some fine silver and glasses fit for emperors.

Good wine, too. The sisters, Millicent and Gertie, knew their wine. They also knew their scotch and resorted to it wordlessly after the best pheasant and lemon pudding I think I've ever eaten.

I said, 'Oh this has been lovely. Lovely.' We stood under the green moon that did not so much light the fells as isolate them in the long clean lines of the faded day.

'You are from Sussex,' said Millicent. 'You must find this very bare.'

'It's wonderful. I love it.'

'I hope you'll stay the winter,' said Gertie. 'And I hope you'll come here soon again.'

The two of them walked, not too steadily to the iron gates and I roared off in the little Fiat down the drive and out on to the fell, between the knobbly blocks of the stone walls flashing up in the car lights. I felt minute between the long lines snaking away, the long low undecorated horizon, the clear hard pencil lines cut with a very sharp hard point. Gigantic lamp-eyes of sheep now and then came shining into the headlights. It was midnight. I did not meet a single car between Mealbeck and Naresby and the road rippled up and down, narrow and sweeping and black and quiet. I thought of Alan in Hong Kong. It would be breakfast time. I wished he were with me. Then I forgot him in the emptiness of the road under the moon and the great encircling ball of the stars.

I went flying through High Thwaite, hurtling through Low Thwaite and the same landscape spread out still in front of me – endlessly deserted, not a light in any cottage, not a dog barking, not a cry of a bird. It was just after what appeared to be the loneliest part of the road that I took a corner rather faster than I should and saw the woman standing in her garden and waving at me with a slow decorous arm, a queenly arm. You could see from the moonlight that her head was piled up high with queenly hair. I think I was about two miles on before I really took it in. I was so shaken by it that I stopped the car.

I was not many miles from home now – my village, my new house, my heavy safe front door. The road had dropped low to a humped bridge, and after a moment when I had switched off the engine I could hear the clear quick brown water running deep and noisy below it. I thought, 'There can't have been anyone. I'm drunk.'

I got out of the car and walked about. It was cold. I stood on the bridge. Apart from the noise of the beck everything was absolutely quiet. There was not a light from any house in any direction. Down here by the beck I could see no horizons, not the fell's edge, not even the sweet nibbled grass beside the road. The air smelled very clean like fresh sheets.

This was the pedlar's road. For five hundred years, they had walked it with packs of ribbons and laces and buttons and medicines, and a great many of them according to all the stories had been murdered for them or disappeared in the snow in winter – often not found until Martinmas. If my car doesn't start now, I thought I shall be very much alone.

Had the woman been asking for help? I wondered whether to go back. I felt absolutely certain – and it is amazing how much even at midnight under only the palest moon the eye can know from the angle of a moving arm – that she hadn't.

She had been waving kindly. Not afraid. Not asking. Not even beckoning. She had been waving in some sort of recognition.

I had never been so frightened in my life.

'I went to Mealbeck last night.'
'Y'd get a fair plateful there.'
'Yes.'
'And a fair skinful.'
'We – yes. Lovely wine.'
'Wine, eh? And mebbe a tot?'
'I had a lovely time. They're very nice. Very kind.'
'That's right. They're kind. Home boozers. Did you get back safe? They say the police sits outside Mealbeck when there's entertaining. When they can spare't time.'

122

'I'm not saying anything against them'

'That's right then.' He – it was the farmer who had the demented dogs and whose wife came from the Danish settlement – he looked satisfied. I could see he had been wondering if I was too fancy to answer back. 'They're right. Old Gertie and Millicent. There's nowt amiss wi' them. Did you have a fair drive home?'

'Fair,' I said, 'One thing wasn't though. I passed a place –. I saw a ghost.'

'Oh aye. Y'd see half a dozen after a night out at Mealbeck.'

'No, I don't think it was that. I saw someone at a gate. It was a woman waving.'

'Oh aye.'

'Well – it was nearly one o'clock in the morning.'

'Did yer stop?' He was clipping. The sheep was taut between his legs, its yellow eyes glaring. The clippers snapped deep into the dirty heathery wool.

'Well, no. I didn't believe it till I was miles past. It took a minute. Then I thought I'd dreamed. Dropped asleep.'

'Woman was it? Dark-haired?'

'I didn't see the colour. Just the shape.'

'Did yer go on back?'

'No – well. She didn't seem to be in trouble or anything. I hope I did right. Not going back.'

He said nothing till the fleece of the sheep fell away and the animal sprang out of his clutches like a soul released and slithered dizzily light into the yard.

'Watch now or yer'll get yerself hiked,' he said as I stood clear. 'The Missus'll have a pot of tea if you fancy it.'

'*Was* it a ghost?'

'Missus!'

She appeared at the door and looked pleased to see me – this really was a wonderfully friendly country – 'Kettle's on', she called. 'I hear yer've bin gallivanting at the Hall.'

'Was it a ghost?' I asked again before I went into tea.

'I'd not think so,' he said.

I went back along the road the very next day and at first I could find no sign of the house at all. Or at any rate I could not decide which one it was. The fell that had looked so bare at night, by daylight could be seen to be dotted with crumpled, squat little stone farms, their backs turned to the view, two trees to each to form a wind-break, grey with white stone slabs to the window and only a tall spire of smoke to show they were occupied. It was not the townsfolk-country-cottage belt so that there was not much white paint about, lined curtains, urns on yard walls – and any one of several little isolated farms could have been the eerie one. In the end I turned back and found the bridge where I'd stopped. I got out of the car again as I had before, and walked back a mile or two until I came to a lane going alongside a garden end. All I could see from the road was the garden end – a stone wall and a gate quite high up above me and behind that a huge slab-stoned roof so low that the farmhouse must have been built deep down in a dip.

Now nobody stood at the gate – more of a look-out post, a signalling post above the road. There were tangled flowers behind it. There was no excuse for me to go up the lane that must have led to the house and it was not inviting. I thought of pretending to have lost my way or asking for a drink of water but these things you grow out of doing. I might perhaps just ask if there were eggs for sale. This was quite usual. Yet I hung back because the lane was dark and overgrown. I sat down instead on a rickety milk platform meant for churns but all stuck through with nettles and which hardly took my weight. It must have been years since any churn was near it. I sat there in the still afternoon and nobody passed.

Then I felt I was being watched. There was no sound or snapping twig, no breathing and no branch stirred but I looked quickly up and into a big bewildered face, mouth a little open, large bright mooning eyes. The hair was waved deeply like an old *Vogue* photograph and the neckline of the dress was rounded, quite high with a string of pearls. The hands of the woman were on the wall and I think they were gloved – neat pretty kid gloves. The trappings of the whole figure were all the very soul of order and confidence. The figure itself, however, almost yearned with uncertainty and loss.

'Whatever *time* is it?' she said.

'About three o'clock.' I found I had stood up and turned to face her. For all the misery in the face there were the relics of unswervable good manners which demanded good manners back; as well as a quite curious sensation, quite without visible foundation, that this body, this dotty half-bemused memsahib had once commanded respect, inspired good sense.

'It's just after three,' I said again.

'Oh, good *gracious* – good gracious.' She turned with a funny, bent movement feeling for the wall to support her as she moved away. The face had not been an old woman's but the stance, the tottering walk were ancient. The dreadful sense of loss, the melancholy, were so thick in the air that there was almost a smell, a sick smell of them.

She was gone, and utterly silently, as if I had slept for a moment in the sunshine and had a momentary dream. She had seemed like a shade, a classical Greek shade, though why I should think of ancient Greece in bleak North Westmorland I did not know.

As I stood looking up at the gate there was a muffled urgent plunging noise and round the bend of the road came sheep – a hundred of them with a shepherd and two dogs. The sheep shouldered each other, fussing, pushing, a stream of fat fleeces pressed together, eyes sharp with pandemonium. The dogs were happily tearing about. The shepherd walked with long steps behind. The sheep new-clipped filled the road like snow. They stopped when they saw me, then when they were yelled at came on careering drunkenly round me, surrounding me and I stood knee deep in them and the flat blank rattle of bleats, the smell of sheep dip and dog and man – and petrol, for when I looked beyond I found a land-rover had been crawling behind and at the wheel the doctor with the tweed hat was sitting laughing.

He said, 'Well! You look terrified.'

'They were so sudden.'

'They'll not hurt you.'

'No. I know – just they were so – quiet. They broke in –'

'Broke in?'

'To the silence. It's very – silent here, isn't it?' I was inane.

He got down from the car and came round near me. 'You've not been here long, have you? We haven't been introduced. I'm the doctor.'

'I know. I'm –'

'Yes. I know too. And we're to know each other better. We're both to go dining out at the good sisters' in a week or so. I gather we're not supposed to know it yet. We are both supposed to be lonely.'

I said how could one be lonely here? I had made friends so fast.

'Some are,' he said. 'Who aren't born to it. Not many. It's always all right at first.' We both looked together towards the high gate and he said, 'Poor Rose. My next patient. Not that I expect to be let in.'

'Is she –?'

'A daughter of the regiment like yourself. Well, I mustn't discuss patients. I call on her now and then.'

He walked up the side lane waving the tweed hat and left me. As he reached the point where the little lane bent out of sight he turned and cheerfully waved again, and I turned too and walked the two miles back to my car. As I reached it the land-rover passed me going very fast and the doctor made no signal and I could not see his face. I thought he must be reckless to drive at that lick on a sheep-strewn road but soon forgot it in the pleasure of the afternoon – the bright fire I'd light at home and the smell of wood smoke and supper with a book ahead. No telephone, thank God. As I turned into my yard I found I was very put out to see Mrs Metcalfe coming across it with yet another great basket of beans.

'Tek 'em or leave 'em,' she said. 'But we've more than we'll want and they'll just get the worm in. Here, you could do wi' a few taties too from the look of you. Oh aye – and I've just heard. That daft woman up near Mealbeck. She's dead. The doctor's just left her. Or I hear tell. She hanged herself.'

It was no story.

Or rather it is the most detestable, inadmissable story. For I don't yet know half the facts and I don't feel I want to invent any. It would be a story so easy to improve upon. There are half a dozen theories about poor Rose's hanging and half a dozen about the reason for her growing isolation and idleness and seclusion. There is only one view about her character though, and that is odd because the whole community in the fells and Dales survives on firmly-grounded assessment of motives and results; the gradations and developments of character are vital to life and give validity to passing years. Reputations change and rise and fall. But Rose – Rose had always been very well-liked and had very much liked living here. Gertie and Millicent said she had fitted in round here as if she were country born. She had been one of the few southerners they said who had seemed to belong. She had loved the house – a queer place. It had been the heart of a Quaker settlement. Panes of glass so thick you could hardly see out. She had grown more and more attached to it. She didn't seem able to leave it in the end.

'The marriage broke up after the War,' said the doctor. We were sitting back after dinner in the housekeeper's room among the Thomas Lawrences. 'He was always on the move. Rose had no quarrel with him you know. She just grew – well, very taken with the place. It was – yes, possession. Greek idea – possession by local gods. The Romans were here you know. They brought a Greek legend or two with them.'

I said, 'How odd, when I saw her I thought of the Greeks, though I hadn't known what I meant. It was the way she moved – so old. And the way she held her hands out. Like, – well, sort of like on the walls of Troy.'

'Not Troy,' said the Doctor. 'More like hell, poor thing. She was quite gone. You know – these fells, all the little isolated houses, I'm not that sure how good for you they are, unless you're farming folk.'

Millicent said rubbish.

'No,' he said, 'I mean it. D'you remember C.S. Lewis's hell? A place where people live in isolation unable to reach each other. Where the houses get further and further apart?'

'Everyone reaches each other here,' I said. 'Surely?'

The doctor was looking at me and I noticed he was looking at me very hard. He said, 'What was it you said?'

'Everyone reaches each other –'

'No,' he said. 'You said you saw her.'

'Yes I did. I saw her on the way home from here, the night before she died. Then I saw her again the next day, the very afternoon. That's what is so terrible. I must have seen her, just before she – did it. I must be the last person to have seen her.'

127

'I wonder,' he said, 'if that could be true.' Gertie and Millicent were busy with coffee cups. They turned away.

' "Could be true?" But it is certainly true. I know exactly when. She asked me the time that afternoon. I told her. It was just after three. She seemed very – bewildered about it. You called upon her hardly a quarter of an hour later. She'd hardly been back in the house a quarter of an hour.'

'She'd been in it longer than that,' he said, 'When I found her she'd been dead for nearly three weeks. Maybe since hay-time.'

I went to Hong Kong.

The Sidmouth Letters

'Lookit, Annie, Lois died.'

'What!'

'Hello? Annie? Lookit, Lois died.'

'When? What?'

'She died. Can you come round here?'

'Of course. Of course. I'll be there at once. Shorty – did you say? You didn't say –?'

'Claridges. Take a cab. Oh, and Annie –'

'Oh Shorty, Shorty!'

'Annie, will you bring a night case? I'm goin' to get you to take a train journey for me.'

So that I was in the train to Axminster, a stifling July midday, with a cheque in my pocket for a thousand pounds and a bag by my side with nightdress and toothbrush in it and my feet on the seat opposite saying, 'No! Lois dead. Dead!'

Yesterday I'd talked all day to her. Drunk as she was we had talked all day. All the way down the Portsmouth Road nearly to Winchester and back, in the hired Mercedes, Shorty driving, oblivious of her with his high-pitched literary friend beside him.

Lois dead.

And I doing Shorty's dirty work.

Yesterday if anyone had told me that I would ever work for Shorty I'd not have believed it.

Nor was it for any love of Lois. Not *love* of Lois. Not even friendship for Lois. I'd hardly known her.

But Lois dead! I lit a cigarette and thought.

I first met Shorty Shenfold years and years ago when I was his student doing a year's course with him on the English Novel at a small university in the Middle West. It was he who had chosen me for the scholarship, gone in to my qualifications with the greatest thoroughness, almost asking – I believe he did ask – for my English birth certificate, my mother's maiden name and the name of even my kindergarten through to my Cambridge College before deciding on me.

He was impressive. He was not I think called Shorty because of his enormous size – no one got affectionate about Shorty – but because of his predilection for the short: short story, short polemic, short but searching criticism, short shrift. Even for an American his style of lecturing was monumentally dull, but even for an American his accuracy and exhaustiveness were remarkable. His slim books which kept appearing at respectable intervals in better and better bindings and at higher and higher prices, while they read like railway timetables, were magnificently thorough. Not a scholar could fault them. Soon they stopped trying. Every conscientious university in the States bought a copy and each was translated excellently into German – rather more curiously into French. Soon they could be seen on the most hallowed shelves in the world where they were taken out and used for reference in academic emergencies about every ten or fifteen years.

Shorty also became known for a side-line: the occasional short controversial piece about the great which he produced for one or other of the more popular literary papers – clever, sharp, always short – and though not exactly scandalous or irresponsible, with the tang of something rather nasty about it. Shorty was, I think, the first to consider Dorothy Wordsworth as anything more than her brother's beloved sister. Long before Anthony Burgess he enthusiastically launched into the syphilitic overtones in the life of Shakespeare. It was said that he had much to suggest, after the fifty years of family grace were up, about Kipling, and his piece on how far Keats had got with Fanny Brawne was discussed for many a furious week in *The Times Literary Supplement*, ensuring that every word of it was widely read. Shorty was a good scholar but his pastimes and tactics were a hyena's.

His looks however were a bull's – a bull's neck, a bull's

crinkly chunk of hair, a bull's manners and a bull's dangerous-
ness, and what in the world made me submit to him, when
I was hardly twenty years old, a piece of my own unsolicited
work about Jane Austen, God alone knows. It was a short piece
which in my innocence I had thought might interest him about
Jane Austen's only – and putative – love affair on a seaside
holiday on the Dorset-Devon coast, the one or two (I forget now)
contemporary hints of it and a history of the later references and
theories. The piece established nothing new at all about 'this
shadowy lover', but I think it was the first time the facts and
allusions had been seriously set out.

It was a short report – the family summer holiday 'by some
sea-side,' probably at Sidmouth, after the loss of the loved
childhood home, Jane Austen's anxiety about her coming life
in Bath, and the first suggestions that she felt she was growing
out of her youth. Then the meeting with the delightful man
'said to be a clergyman' (some said a sailor, some a doctor),
thought even by her formidable sister to have 'been worthy of
Jane.' Then the man's sudden departure, 'called away on family
business', and three weeks later the roundabout, astonishing
news of his death. I examined all of it as best I could, then the
return of the family to Bath and the final move to Chawton;
Jane Austen's eventual new strength there after three years of
utter silence; her increased interest in and love for her young
nephews and nieces as they grew up, the desk in the window of
the unremarkable sitting room looking out at the unremarkable
view; the procession of the five great books, the new spectacular
sympathy and good sense about love which have ever since
comforted the world.

I called the thing something too pompous – *Jane Austen –
Love and Privacy* – I dare say, and it was no doubt as bad and
unscholarly as the title. I lost it long ago so I can't tell. But, no
doubt through Shenfold's training, I believe it was thorough
and properly set out, and when he handed it back to me with
only a tick and 'interesting' on it and passed me out with a very
poor grade at the end of my year and hardly – though I was his
own particular choice of student from England – hardly a
goodbye, I was very disappointed.

I was surprised, therefore, about a year later, to read under the title *Jane Austen at Sidmouth* and over his name, my article word for word with just the added hint that the lover's disappearance was a little mysterious, more of a getaway than a death. Don't ask me how this was done, but the suggestion was certainly there and his, as the rest of the work was undoubtedly mine.

I watched Shorty's flight up the ladder with some interest after that. I even met him again once or twice in England over the years. The first time was by chance outside the London Library. It was about five years after his piece on the Sidmouth lover, but he recognised me and I think would have pretended not to had I not called out 'Oh!'

He invited me to his flat at Brook Street – a party that same evening – where Fellows of All Souls put their finger tips together and stared into space, and several lady novelists looked out of windows.

He was as ebullient as ever – the perfect host, eyes everywhere. Food, drink, waiters all superb. His clothes – never a whiter shirt, a suit more English – must have cost a bomb and had pretty clearly not been paid for out of his grants and scholarships and awards, though even when I first knew him his powers of negotiating an award would have been of use to any multi-national oil company. All – I heard from one of the lady novelists – had been provided by a series of wives.

Now at first looking at Shorty one was a bit uncertain about wives. It was not that he looked homosexual – he had a big brown juicy glare for any woman who came his way – but he had the homosexual's awareness of himself and his image that does not go with conventional sexual diversion. His big, slow, lumbering frame making its way across the Ritz or Claridges – I was invited to meet him there now and then after he had begun to hear of my books – spoke of a spiffing physical and mental health, a supreme self-confidence, but not what my cousin Enid calls, 'the life upstairs.' For to Shorty – so they said in *Private Eye* and I am sure to his delight, 'Excitement means the pen.'

There must have been a certain type of woman who responded to him, however, because several of them married him. I met one in Brook Street, then there was a second – I saw her pictures in the evening papers sometimes – and then there was Lois. All three were much the same – tall, dreamy, bony, American good-looking with a tiny bewildered voice and a gigantic bank balance. Women who had the air of people needing a good rest. How he got hold of them nobody knows but it was surmised by the same private and industrious bludgeoning he accorded the short story or the sonnet. A short story or a sonnet bludgeoned by Shorty looked as if it needed a good rest, too, and usually got one.

One Thursday, two days before our outing to Chawton down the Portsmouth Road and three days before my mission with the thousand pound cheque, I had met Shorty again after another long interval. It was a summer afternoon meeting of the Royal Soceity of Literature in Hyde Park Gate with all the trees blowing leaves along the Bayswater Road and the clink of tea-cups on the terrace. There he sood – not aged a bit – a great block of a man still, perhaps slightly heavier, perhaps a shade more authoritative if that were possible. He towered above Lord Butler. Lord Snow became a flake. His bold brown eyes stuck out, the brains almost bursting from the bull's forehead. When he spoke it was still with the surprising coarse, slow snarl so different from the rest of him that it seemed an affectation.

Near him, looking out over the balustrade, hung Lois, more raddled than I remembered but bird-boned, huge-eyed, expensive still. Her fingers were knobbed with rings, her old frail feet were in crocodileskin, like prickly silk. As I saw her she turned and began to walk towards the lecture room where people were beginning to settle on the canvas chairs. I followed and said, 'Lois.'

She said, 'Well, hi,' and slid to the floor in the path of the Duchess of Kent. (For it was a big occassion and prizes were being handed out.)

'I'm pissed,' said Lois loud and clear as the Duchess stepped over her, and Shorty and I got her back to Claridges where we called a doctor, had a bit of a battle with the gin bottle and eventually put her to bed.

Shorty managed splendidly. Not even whilst holding his poor wife's head in Hyde Park Gate – I at the other end with the crocodile shoes – did he lose his dignity, and afterwards he rang me up and in the same grating, metallic voice as of old asked me if I would go out with them on Saturday. Yep – she was quite better. Yep – it happened often. It was an illness, poor Lois. He preferred to treat it as an illness. Now then. Lois had especially asked for me to go. Also, I would be useful, Lois not being able to be left at home. We would be going with a very famous man – a literary journalist often to be seen on the box. Yep – that's the man. And lookit – I knew the guy he was sure. He suspected that I knew all the big names now lookit (and here I did just wonder if I felt the slightest pause), we would be going to Chawton, near Winchester. To photograph some handwriting. Ya. Yep. Thassit. Jane Austen's cottage. And we'd have lunch somewhere.

I had not the least wish in the world to go. I felt that in some mysterious way Shorty Shenfold was haunting me. Why, of all the people I had met in my life, was it Shenfold who kept turning up? And what had happed to all the dear old friends, the ones who in novels are suddenly there in the street beside you, dancing to the music of time? Why for me was there only unspeakable Shenfold? And why could I never say no?

The photographic session was to be at the Chawton cottage on the Saturday morning before it was open to the public – a pre-arranged and rather stately affair. A senior member of the Jane Austen Society was in attendance. We were warmly welcomed and Lois and I allowed to watch the whole ceremony. I was allowed to hold the MSS, touch the old writing paper, smell it, look close at the lovely, diamond-sharp, unmistakable hand.

Lois was soon bored and wandered away into the living-room, and I heard the clatter of an Austen-type vegetable dish displayed on the Austen-type dining table and thought I'd better go after her.

She stood by the writing desk in the window drawing an old woman's finger over the old blotched wood. Only the hands showed her to be twenty years older than Shorty – her figure was ageless, American East Coast, face fragile, cherished, painted; she looked out at the Chawton pub across the village street and blinked her wet blue eyes. She said, 'So she jus' sat here, did she? Writin' away?'

I said that this was what was said.

'So she looked right in at the pub, did she?'

I said that I supposed so. It was an old pub. The cottage itself had once been a pub, but the pub across the road was quite old too. She might have sat at an angle, I said, facing the pond that used to be over towards what was the car park now – on the right.

'The pond or the pub,' said Lois. 'Like me, it's the pond or the pub.'

'Not with Jane Austen,' I said. 'She never despaired.'

'Don't they say she sat in a hood? Right over her face? Near the end? When her face – her terrible discoloured face . . . ?'

I said that I had read about that somewhere. It had been a caul not a hood.

'The pond or the pub in a caul. Jesus,' said Lois. 'Poor bitch. Y'know, Annie, I wonder what she really felt?'

She took a scent bottle out of her bag and swigged at it.

'She never met anyone like me, did she? Don't seem to me she knew a lot. I bet she'd never even looked inside that pub.'

She began to cry.

'Someone ought a write a book about me,' she said, 'not about this bitch. About me. Dare say they will. Some hard-mouthed boring bitch. Some frienda Shorty. Shorty likes a hard-mouthed bitch. Write her up. Lot this bitch knew –'

Shorty and the literary editor were coming towards the living room. Before they had seen us I heard the literary editor say in the little connecting lobby, 'My dear – this is going to be *utterly* exciting.'

Then we got Lois back into the Mercedes and to London. She was not well enough for luncheon in Hampshire and nobody seemed to mind except me – I was hungry. Shorty and the literary young man had much to say to each other in the front of the car and I spent the mercifully fast journey in the back trying to command the scent bottle. It was a long afternoon. The following morning Shorty rang to say Lois was dead.

I had been afraid that when I got to Claridges I would not be able to stand him – or anything. I expected possessions in heaps, splayed suitcases (she had been hideously untidy), even twisted sheets – the Manager with hooded eyes, Shorty calm as ever but ashen, and a smell – her scent, her gin, her cigarettes, her hectic presence still about.

It was almost as unnerving to meet with no shadow or breath of a memory of her. Through the door of the suite leading to the bedroom I saw twin beds at a distance from each other under splendid dark quilts. The flowers were fresh, cupboards all firmly closed, an ice bucket and polished glasses on a tray. The *Observer* neatly folded.

Shorty, dressed for the city though in rather an unusually dark tie, opened the door. He was in great command. I saw as he kissed me – the kiss for funerals, excusable now if never again – that he had carefully considered the coming interview. Everything was ready in his head, another part of his work dealt with and completed. 1. – he had thought – Ring Annie. 2. Look up trains for Axminster. 3. Notes for Annie, payment etc., 4. Kiss on arrival.

'She died in the night. It had been expected.' he said, 'Sit down. Have a dr – coffee?'

'I'm very sorry, Shorty,' I said when the coffee had come.

He said, 'It was bad, but quick.'

'Quick? I thought perhaps years.'

'Oh – she'd been – ill – for years. But quick last night. They dealt with it very well here. Very well. Better at night of course. Hotel. It's gotta cost somethin' –'

I shut my eyes.

'Stretcher. Ambulance. Christ.'

'Yes.'

'Now of course I get the rough stuff. Cables. Funerals.'

'Haven't you *sent* cables?'

'Oh ya. Yep. Comin' right over. Big family. New York. Comin' here. There's goin' to be big troubles with the will. I've had a lot to do there.' He looked quickly at me, bewildered and I saw in him the confusion I had felt yesterday. He was thinking, 'Why her? Why does she keep cropping up? Why do I tell her?'

'Was Lois – did Lois have children?'

'Nope. Give thanks. Only child, too. Said she'd always wanted a sister. You'd not have thought, to look –'

'Lookit,' he said, 'could you do somethin' for me? I don't want journalists in on this, so I ask you.'

I thought of the tick and 'interesting' and the poor degree he

136

had given me – his scant goodbye. Then of *Jane Austen at Sidmouth*. But then of the brave crocodile shoes, the fragile old feet, the trembling old hand on the Austen dinner service. She had wanted a sister. I said, 'Anything I can.'

He sat down at the desk and became at once the professor. He moved papers about, sighed, touched a pen, a pile of notes. He straightened them. His bulging eyes looked only down.

'It is right up your street, Annie, if I remember. Something that cropped up. I'll let you in on it. I've let a newspaper in on it – that chap yesterday who talks on the box – but only up to a point. They're paying expenses so you can make 'em high. The American and European rights are about fixed up. I've already spat it at my publisher.'

'What is it?'

'Well, it's Jane Austen. Jane Austen again. I've been doing a bit of work lately. Lois – Lois and I – we spent a bit of time down in Sidmouth, Devon. Teignmouth, Lyme, Starcross, Portsmouth – those places. We found – lookit, Annie, this is just between ourselves and naturally you gonna get paid – we found a link with Sidmouth. The Sidmouth holiday. 1801. The Sidmouth lover.'

'A link?'

'Yes.' The quick, uneasy look again as if there were something more to be said, something missing he felt he should know. 'There's a link. There's still a link. Near Sidmouth. The three silent years. The "shadowy lover".'

'You have found that he existed?'

'We have found –' said Shorty Shenfold – he spread great big pink pads of hands on the desk and leaned back. His huge face looked hot. After the rigours of the night he had shaved perfectly, his teeth shone. Tie, collar, hair, everything were immaculate but he seemed sweaty. 'There is every probability,' he said, 'That there are several letters by Jane Austen to the lover still in Devonshire and for sale.'

I said nothing and he went on, 'For sale today. At an address I'll give you, Annie. I've arranged to meet the woman at three o'clock and to pay a thousand pounds. I've worked up to this for more than a year – longer. Then the whole thing gells in a week. It had to be this week.'

'Gells?'

137

'I got an answer – a favourable answer – from the woman who looks after the – owner of the letters. In the end I got her to say the owner – it's her grandmother – would see me. She says there is a small bundle of Jane Austen's letters – they're always been called that – her grandmother keeps in some box. The grandmother is the great granddaughter of the woman who kept the Sidmouth – or whatever it was – lodging-house. Presumably they were letters from Austen sent to the lover to wait his return. He died and they were never delivered. The bundle is only known within the family. It's become some sort of tailisman – household god.'

'If they're unopened,' I said, 'how do you know they're not a laundry list?'

'Yep. It's a risk. But worth it. The money is – was – not all that important. Get it paid over today – it's predated – and we'll not have to put it in the estate. Lois was loaded.

'So would you go, Annie? It's not Sidmouth any more. It's Charmouth – just down the coast. Probably why they've not been discovered – dead-an-alive place. Worse than the rest, which is pushin' it. You can see Lyme from there. It's Austen heartland. Maybe you'll like it. All you do is explain why I can't be there myself. I'll give you a letter. I'll telephone, too, if it's possible to get a moment.'

'Do you want me to read them?'

For the first and only time I felt sorry for Shorty. He took almost half a minute to reply. The look came again – maybe if he had not just passed the night he had passed he would have been able to hide it, but he looked quickly, sharply at me as if he were afraid. Afraid that there were something that for once in its career his splendid computer's brain had missed. And there was something else that made me for that quick moment like him – he was genuinely, genuinely longing to see the bundle, to be the first to hold the beautiful, live writing in his hand.

Yet if they were nothing? A laundry list?

A thousand pounds was from today going to be a thousand pounds. Lois's tired old claws would be writing no more cheques.

'Well, you'd better look at them,' he said at length. 'Read them. They'll be all right. I'm pretty sure. They say they've never been read. Don't sound so likely, but you never know. Sound a queer lot, this family.'

'Get back tonight if you can. Bring them here. Take a taxi soon as you get back to Waterloo. Here's twenty pounds in case you have to stay over, but try to get back. There'll be other pay later of course.'

'I shan't need paying, Shorty.'

He looked at me with utter hatred because I did not need paying and because I was going to see the letters – and again the troubled look. A ripple of pure annoyance went across the big bumpy forehead, not a thought, nor even quite a feeling; a sort of intuitive shadow that there was something he had missed, something he should have spotted all those years ago when he had looked in to my background before giving me the scholarship to his college in America; when I had written my piece on *Love and Privacy*.

Which there was. He had forgotten that on my application form it had said where I was born and had lived with my family for twenty years. In 'Austen heart-land'. At Sidmouth.

Enid saw me through the window before I even rang the bell and I saw her purse up her lips in the old way as she made for the door. She said, 'Well, Annie,' mouth still tight. There was a fan of lines round her mouth now. She had always pursed her lips when she was trying not to show excitement. It had left a map.

She had grown fatter. Her hair was grey but very neatly permed and set. She wore a home-made linen dress over an acreage of bust. Pearl earrings and a brooch. Presumably all for Shenfold.

'We expected an American professor and we get you. Well Annie. It's a very long time.'

'Did he telephone?'

'Who? Telephone? Oh – no. This is some mad American professor trying to offer us a fortune for Gran's bundle.'

'He said he'd try to telephone.'

'You know him? Goodness, Annie, you're not something to do with it? Anyway, come in.'

The tremendous noise of a racing commentary at full throttle came through the closed sitting-room door. 'Come in the kitchen,' she said. 'I'll make tea. I'm not waiting for this scrounger any longer.'

'Is Auntie –?'

'In the sitting-room. Sleeps there too now. She feels the cold. And the telly's in there. I never bother with it.'

'Feels the cold *today*!'

'Yes. You look hot, old Annie. D'you want to go and wash? Did you come by car?'

'No. Train and bus. The train was late. And boiling.'

I saw her think that I had no car and that I probably hadn't much of a life otherwise. No proper job, no marriage, only four or five novels in goodness knows how many years. Bits of reviewing. Something insignificant and part-time for the British Council. And after such a good start. Cambridge, then America. She, Enid, had left school at sixteen. She touched her pearls and said, 'We liked your last book. Well, we've liked them all, Gran and I. Why don't you write more? Something easy and rambly. People round here like them very much you know. They often try and get them out of the library, but it takes so long.'

'I'm slow too.'

'You usen't to be. I'm sure you could write a big book. D'you remember what a lot you used to write when we were little? Uncle couldn't keep you in notebooks.'

'Those were the days. Whizzing along with nothing to say. And no problems.'

'Problems?' Her eyes asked me to tell her my problems and then looked away with understanding that they were mine. I thought how much I liked my cousin and had always liked her. I wondered why I didn't come down here often – her comforting goodness, this quiet house, sideways to the sea in the seaside garden, the same french doors still open on to the unpainted, bleached balcony where we had poured sand out of our shoes before meals when I had been over to stay as a child. The sound of the sea loud and lively down the lane.

'No – I mean writing problems. There were none then. At ten you just go on and on. It's not like later. It's fuss, fuss, later – a few pages. Then disgust. Looking out of the window, up at the soles of all the feet going by.'

'*Up* at the feet! Good gracious, it's time you were down here, Annie. Whyever don't you come back? For a good long time? We're very quiet. I'm rather –,' she put out cups and saucers on a trolley with the greatest appearance of self-sufficiency and produced a huge home-made cake from a tin, 'I'm rather lonely I suppose really. Gran's a jolly good laugh of course.'

'She must be ninety,' I said.

'She's ninety-six.'

'Is she well?'

'She's very well. The memory comes and goes a bit. Patchy you know. Like a loose connection. But yes, she's very well. Why don't you come back? Home and family and all that. After all, they meant a lot to our own famous loose connection didn't they? Her family never stopped her from writing books – she lived for them, didn't she? Made all the jam.' I noticed Enid's great big bossy jaw again. I said, 'The Austens weren't just any family,' and felt penitent at once when she blushed, hurt.

'Neither are we just any family. The Austens were very clever – Oxford and Cambridge and Admirals and so on – but nothing out of the way socially. The story goes that to meet them they were nothing out of the way at all.'

I said, 'You're like the Irish, still going on about a hundred and fifty years ago. The Austen thing's a legend, Enid. Thank goodness we've always kept it to ourselves and never got shown up about it. It's nonsense. We've all been told for generations that Jane Austen's lover once put up at some old auntie's boarding house. There are one or two anecdotes and the famous unopened bundle. Years ago someone should have written a monograph. It's all probably rubbish.'

'I always thought you would write a monograph.'

'I did write something once. If anyone had taken any notice of it I suppose I'd have written more. I didn't put anything in it that was family gossip though.'

'What?'

'I gave it to my American professor. The year I was out there. I hoped he'd ask to talk about it but he just put a tick and said "interesting".'

'Well, it was quite good of him to do that if you put nothing new in it.'

'I didn't know anything new. Nothing definite. Just yarns. "Jane Austen was so happy" – that stuff.'

'"Merry",' said Enid, 'not happy. They always said merry. That's what I was brought up on. "Miss Austen and Miss Jane Austen called and Miss Jane Austen was merry."'

'Maybe she'd been at the bottle.'

'Annie!'

'There you go,' I said. 'Jane-worship. And I'll bet you haven't read one of the novels in years.'

'Jane Austen at the bottle! She never had any experience of that sort of person.'

I thought of Lois and said, 'Then she was extremely fortunate.'

'She was sensible about misfortune,' said Enid. 'She was thankful for compensations. She was a respectable woman and at a guess I'd say she was very sensible about all the excesses – love and passion and that sort of thing. It's one of the reasons I would – yes, I don't care what we've always said – I would like to read what's in Gran's bundle.'

'Which is why you've decided to sell it to Shorty Shenfold?'

'I didn't decide. He pestered away – you never saw such letters he wrote. Solid paragraphs. Bright blue type and paper half an inch thick.'

'Enid, you don't *need* the money.'

'No. But he sounds respectable. Scholarly. He wrote from Claridges. And he seems to think it is very important. Well, haven't we a duty when you think about it to read what's in the packet? But I certainly hadn't made up my mind.'

'He told me,' I said, 'that you had. And the sale was as good as made.'

'Rubbish. I've hardly mentioned it to Gran yet. I said he could come down and see her if he liked. Anyway, it seems to me that you must have a lot to do with this yourself.'

'You won't believe it, but he hasn't the faintest idea I even know you.'

'You mean,' said Enid, looking down her nose as she had done when telling me that the Austens were nothing socially out of the way, 'You mean that he doesn't know that we are *cousins*!'

142

She pushed the trolley ahead of us in to the sitting-room where two exhausted horses were neck and neck and the commentator on the verge of apoplexy. A huddled person pounded the arms of its chair with small blotchy brown claws. The heavy curtains were drawn across the window for a better appreciation of Sandown Park and a huge fire roared in the grate. My great aunt, Enid's great grandmother, was surrounded by her tools and weapons – a couple of walking sticks, a long picker, several rugs, a box of sweets and a huge black handbag bulging like some old ship come home from the wars. Its ancient cracked sides and loose old tortoiseshell handles brought such a rush of memory I had to sit down – (Annie, here blow your nose. Stop crying, Annie, here's a Mars bar. No need to run for plasters, Enid, here's my bag. Yes, *and* iodine.) I sat down quickly close to her.

'Here's Annie, Gran.'

'Good,' said my great aunt, 'I'd five to one on that one.' She wrote something in a notebook. 'Did well in the Oaks,' she told me looking across. 'What's this then? The American professor?'

'No – it's Annie. The professor isn't coming. His wife died.'

'Why should Annie come then? She looks poorly. Smokes too much. Can't think what she wants with London. Writing those books.'

'She's come about your bundle.'

'Why can't she write her books down here, that's what I want to know,' said Auntie and looked deep in the black bag. She came up with a queer-looking packet of sweets. 'D'you want a humbug, Annie?'

'No thanks, Auntie.'

'That professor sounds a humbug. What d'you want to be working for a humbug for? You could have been a professor yourself if you'd wanted. Could have been anything. I often tell Enid, Annie was the clever one. Could have been anything. She used to write that easy. She might have been writing really well-known books by now, full of descriptions.'

'Annie's not exactly working for him –'

'I dare say she writes *clever* books. Though I've never agreed with that either – for all the *Times Littery Whatsit*. They can't

143

be that clever, I said to Enid, or I wouldn't understand them. Turn the sound down. Annie dear, till the next race. I can't do with him splurging and yattering.'

I turned it down and the quiet was a blessing.

'Jane Austen didn't leave home,' said Auntie chewing a humbug and watching the commentator's silent agitations. 'Never too grand to go and stay with her relations. That's the tale we were always told anyway.'

'There were plenty of them,' I said. 'Everyone could take turn and turn about. Nowadays –'

'What's nowadays?' said my great aunt. 'I've seen a good deal of nowadays and it's never any different. What's this professor after? Does he want to marry you?'

'*No!*'

'All right. I've never thought it much mattered anyway. Enid never married – never wanted to. She's all right. I married and I never stopped wishing I hadn't. Mind, Annie should have married. She never tells us anything. I tell her it doesn't matter. She'll always be Annie.'

'I always liked Annie,' she said to Enid. 'I wonder what happened to her? Why don't she ever come and see us?'

'She's here, Gran.'

'This?' She looked at me. 'No, this young woman is an American professor.'

'It's Annie.'

'Annie was always my favourite,' she told me. 'Here. Come here.' She jerked her wispy head backwards a couple of times for me to come closer. She looked like a cunning old bookie. 'Enid's a good woman,' she said. 'We get on and she's a very good girl to me, but Annie – oh Annie was the clever one. It's a tragedy about Annie. I don't know who it was or what went wrong. All she does is write these very good books. Books that get wonderful mentions. The kind you'd never see in any shops –'

'Gran!'

'I'm leaving the money to Enid,' said Auntie, 'and I'm leaving the letters to Annie.'

'Gran, this is what Annie's here for. The professor's sent her with some huge cheque – a thousand pounds. I told you about it.'

144

'I never agreed.'

'No. I know you didn't. Neither did I. I never said we'd sell the things but –'

'I should hope not. They've been in this family since Lizzie's mother's gran.' She stretched out with the long picker and twitched the television into life. The sound of the next race shook the room. A board stating odds filled the screen. Gran said, 'Anyway, a thousand's under-priced.'

When the race was over – it seemed again to have been to her advantage – she said, 'Trying to get them cheap. American professor!'

I said, 'Auntie, it's very good of you. It would be wonderful to have the letters.'

'Not to sell, mind. We've never sold them. It's a tradition. And it's a tradition we've never looked at them.'

'No. Of course not.'

'They're not to be read.'

'Gran,' said Enid, 'Annie might take advice about that. You know it may be the time has come –'

'No. No. They're not to be read. It says on the packet who they're for. He never came for them. You don't read other folk's letters. Postcards maybe.'

'Auntie –'

'It says who they're for on the envelopes.'

'Then you've looked?'

She began to show the bag again.

'Gran, have you opened the bundle?'

'I've read the fronts of the envelopes, that's all,' and she brought out a very small and thin paper package wrapped in oilskin.

'It's been wrapped in oilskin since long since. Like a baccy pouch. Ever since Lizzie's mother's gran. Nobody came for it. Mind you she moved soon after, Lizzie's mother's gran. She moved here from Sidmouth. She kept it on her mantelpiece a long while, troubled about it. Lizzie's mother grew up with it. She always thought of it as something to do with the sea, being in oilskin.'

I said, 'Maybe they were written to a sailor. Some people say the young man was a sailor. Jane Austen loved sailors,' – and was surprised by a shining hard look, steady and shrewd from under Auntie's eyebrows. My heart began to beat fast. I said, 'It's terribly hot in here. I'm sorry. Look I must go outside,' and she said, 'Well here then, Annie,' and tossed the little packet in to my lap. 'It's yours by rights,' she said. 'I've always felt it. That American can do without it. Have it now. Why wait till I'm dead? It's yours, Annie, being bookish.'

'Will you come back, Annie?'

Enid and I were on the verandah. I was writing to Shorty – very fast to catch the next post – saying that it had all been a mistake. The letters if they still existed were not for sale. They had been given to a relative and – lost track of. He might like to come and talk about it to the family but I felt it was too late.

'You are writing fast. Like old times.'

I said I was just enclosing the cheque, saying it was all off and that if he liked – did she mind? – that he could come down and see for himself.

'Yes of course,' she said. 'There's probably nothing in the packet you can still read anyway. Poor Gran. And poor Annie! It's not much of an inheritance. All this secrecy and I'll bet it's a hoax. I mean she'd have got them back, wouldn't she – Jane Austen? She'd have moved heaven? Her love letters?'

'You'd think so,' I said, 'It depends what sort of a state she was in. We can't tell – there was a family silence about it. We won't find the truth about that now.'

'If they are Jane Austen's letters, Annie, will they – would they – honestly mean anything much?'

'They would be a terrific find,' I said.

'Would they?'

'Yes. Written when she was in love. The critics would go wild. Her sister burned everything to do with that time you know. There's not a letter, not a scratch of Jane Austen's pen for three years. We don't even know the man's name. It was Jane Austen's wish – so it's said. She wanted no speculation. No sharing.'

'But d'you think anyone – the sister, us – has the right to destroy –?'

'Cassandra knew her sister.'

146

'She didn't know her sister was a – well, a genius. She didn't know how famous she was going to be.'

I said I didn't think that would have made the least difference.

Enid came to the gate with me and stood leaning on it. The honeysuckle hedge beside her smelled of nutmeg. Behind her the verandah doors stood open and beyond them and within could be heard the fanfare announcing the television evening news, full strength for Auntie.

'I wish you were nearer, Annie.'

'I wish I were, too. I've loved today. It's just that in London there's more chance – oh, of meeting up with old friends I suppose.'

'A melancholy situation. Depending on people from the past.'

I said, 'Could I come down in the autumn – for a long time, three weeks or so?' and she looked so thrilled that I at once felt hostile, manipulated. I said, 'Well anyway a fortnight,' hating myself. The old guilt was back, the old problem, the hostility, the fight between love and privacy.

Enid blew her nose very thoroughly and said, 'There's a good little hairdresser down here, too. You could get your hair done properly. And there's quite a lot of Bridge.'

She touched the pearls.

When she had gone in I walked to the end of the lane, but then I turned left to the sea instead of right to the bus-stop which would direct me somewhere or other for the night. I walked along the sands, weaving through the sandcastles and spades, the families gathered together in clumps on rugs, over splendid drains and moats and driftwood bridges, over and beyond the spatter of paper cups and tin cans spilling from litter bins, beyond the tussocks of grey-green grass, towards the sand hills and the cliffs.

The sand hills were nearly empty now – people were dragging back to their high tea, tired and sandy and hot I sat looking at the sea as it tilted slowly from the sun. The ripples thickened and the waves seemed to grow slow, soften, breathe more deep. I opened the old sea-weed envelope and read the two envelopes within, the unmistakable handwriting clearer even than yesterday's at Chawton. I opened each envelope and read the signature which was as expected and then I burned both letters and both envelopes with my cigarette lighter.

Then I sat for goodness knows how long, but the sun was nearly gone by the time I came back to myself, so I think it must have been several hours. I took the half-handful of ash down to the water's edge and paddled a fairway out and scattered it. Jane Austen had very much liked Charmouth Bay. 'The happiest spot,' she said, 'for watching the flow of the tide, for sitting in unwearied contemplation.' I let a very small wisp of her melt into it.

That night I fell asleep in a bed-and-breakfast place at Sidmouth utterly certain that I had done right. I woke in the night and I still felt certain. And I have not changed my mind. I have felt very happy ever since that I of all people have had the chance of paying back a little of a great debt.

I haven't seen Shorty again. He didn't answer my letter, though he did go down to Charmouth to try his luck with Auntie. Enid said it was not a success. He got nowhere, Auntie insisting that he was a member of the C.I.A. or the President of the United States for whom it seems she has little time.

Nor has he written to me, but he is alive and well, for last Christmas, when I was down with Enid, she suddenly spotted him in an old *Tatler and Queen*. She sat upright and said 'Gracious!' – and there he was, unchanged, after all these years. He was in Dublin, lecturing on something unpleasant he had discovered about Yeats, and beside him, in the glorious parkland surrounding her house, was a gaunt and beautiful American-Irish widow.

Shenfold looked splendid – hair a thought longer, just a touch of grey, still vigorous, vibrant, an Olympian. Good for another thirty years.

'He's attractive,' said Enid. 'Powerful. You can see he's never missed a thing. Doesn't the woman look tired?'

FAITH FOX

Jane Gardam

'Terribly funny and clever . . . the best thing she's done'
Victoria Wood

When sweet, healthy, hearty Holly Fox dies suddenly in childbirth, the
Surrey village whose pearl she was reverberates with shock. She leaves
behind her a helpless, silent husband, and a tiny daughter, Faith. Everyone
assumes Holly's loving and capable mother Thomasina will look after
Faith, but when she unaccountably deserts her newborn grandchild, the
baby must be packed off to her father's peculiar family in the North –
'the very strangest people you ever saw, my dear'.

With wisdom, generosity and understanding, Jane Gardam takes as her
subject the English heart in all its eccentric variety. *Faith Fox* sheds a clear,
true light on the misery of bereavement and the joyous possibility
of a new beginning.

'Has quite as sharp a take on modern times as *Trainspotting* . . . if you're
too hip for Jane Gardam, then you're too hip'
D.J. Taylor, *New Statesman*

'Funny and admirable . . . Jane Gardam writes with a dark and buoyant
energy which continually challenges and provokes' *The The Times*

'Dazzling . . . Funny, bleak and full of wisdom, *Faith Fox* is a
complete delight'
Marie Claire

'She has Alan Bennett's gift of bringing out the hubris, and,
simultaneously, the humility of her characters, who are
an endearing lot'
Guardian

ABACUS
978-0-349-12101-7

BLACK FACES, WHITE FACES

Jane Gardam

'Very good indeed . . . she writes so well'
Victoria Glendinning

In this loosely connected sequence of short stories, Jane Gardam offers
dazzling vignettes of human foibles in the smilingly fierce
holiday island of Jamaica.

Mrs Filling sees something nasty in the midday sun; an English lawyer
dallies with Mrs Santamania the Bolivian Queen while his wife goes
quietly mad in England; an ancient American silenced by a stroke is
tortured by the ramblings of his wife. Years of studiously correct
behaviour in a colder climate give way to astonishing desires; middle-
aged ladies appear in the wrong clothes; sexuality flares towards the
wrong partners, and everywhere terror, farce and undercurrents of
racial tension lurk beside the swimming pool.

'Jane Gardam has taken the form of the short story as close to art
as it is ever likely to reach'
Peter Ackroyd, *Spectator*

'Extraordinary . . . Jane Gardam is a writer of original spirit, her
observations acute and funny/sad'
Angela Huth, *Guardian*

'She writes like a modern Katherine Mansfield . . . a little gem'
Daily Mail

ABACUS
978-0-349-11407-1

To buy any of our books and to find out
more about Abacus and Little, Brown, our authors
and titles, as well as events and book clubs,
visit our website

www.littlebrown.co.uk

and follow us on Twitter

@AbacusBooks
@LittleBrownUK

To order any Abacus titles p & p free in the UK,
please contact our mail order supplier on:

+ 44 (0)1832 737525

Customers not based in the UK should contact
the same number for appropriate postage
and packing costs.